CLEAR BLUE SKY

LOVE IN THE ADIRONDACKS
BOOK FOUR

JEN TALTY

JUPITER PRESS

This book is a work of fiction. Names, characters, places, and incidents are products of the author's imagination or used fictitiously. Any resemblance to actual events or locales or persons living or dead is entirely coincidental.

Copyright © 2022 by Jen Talty All rights reserved.

No part of this work may be used, stored, reproduced or transmitted without written permission from the publisher except for brief quotations for review purposes as permitted by law.
This book is licensed for your personal enjoyment only. This book may not be re-sold or given away to other people. If you would like to share this book with another person, please purchase an additional copy for each recipient. If you're reading this book and did not purchase it, or it was not purchased for your use only, please purchase your own copy.

CLEAR BLUE SKY
LOVE IN THE ADIRONDACKS, BOOK 4

Love in the Adirondacks, Book 4

USA Today Bestseller
JEN TALTY

PRAISE FOR JEN TALTY

"Deadly Secrets is the best of romance and suspense in one hot read!" *NYT Bestselling Author Jennifer Probst*

"A charming setting and a steamy couple heat up the pages in a suspenseful story I couldn't put down!" *NY Times and USA today Bestselling Author Donna Grant*

"Jen Talty's books will grab your attention and pull you into a world of relatable characters, strong personalities, humor, and believable storylines. You'll laugh, you'll cry, and you'll rush to get the next book she releases!" Natalie Ann USA Today Bestselling Author

"I positively loved *In Two Weeks*, and highly recommend it. The writing is wonderful, the story is fantastic, and the characters will keep you coming back for more. I can't wait to get my hands on future installments of the NYS Troopers series." *Long and Short Reviews*

"*In Two Weeks* hooks the reader from page one. This is a fast paced story where the development of the romance grabs you emotionally and the suspense keeps you sitting on the edge of your chair. Great characters, great writing, and a believable plot that can be a warning to all of us." *Desiree Holt, USA Today Bestseller*

"*Dark Water* delivers an engaging portrait of wounded hearts as the memorable characters take you on a healing journey of love. A mysterious death brings danger and intrigue into the drama, while sultry passions brew into a believable plot that melts the reader's heart. Jen Talty pens an entertaining romance that grips the heart as the colorful and dangerous story unfolds into a chilling ending." *Night Owl Reviews*

"This is not the typical love story, nor is it the typical mystery. The characters are well rounded and interesting." *You Gotta Read Reviews*

"*Murder in Paradise Bay* is a fast-paced romantic thriller with plenty of twists and turns to keep you guessing until the end. You won't want to miss this one..." *USA Today bestselling author Janice Maynard*

To my family.

1

Nelson Snow leaned against the post on the main docks and stared out over the clear blue sky. The sun's rays reached down into Lake George, New York's brilliant waters like a bright glow stick. Considering it was early spring, the lunch crowd was in full swing thanks to an early winter thaw. April in these parts could be freezing, or it could be like today. Sunny and sixty.

He enjoyed the changing of the seasons, so he'd take either as long as he didn't have to deal with the past.

Only today, the past walked right through his front door, reminding him that it lurked in the shadows. There was no hiding from what had happened.

The chatter coming from Blue Moon filled the air. This hadn't been his dream career. It started as a tribute to the men who died during his last mission.

However, since the grand opening, it had become his passion. He couldn't imagine being anywhere else, doing anything else, or working with anyone other than his two brothers.

They had fought like dogs over the restaurant's name. Nelson wanted it to be *Operation Moon*, but both Phoenix and Maverick reminded him that the United States government might take issue with that. The second name he'd come up with had been *Under the Moon*. It wasn't horrible, but his brother Phoenix tossed out *Blue Moon* during a camping trip the first time they visited the area. The moon had this blue glow and Phoenix had been commenting on how spectacular and calming it was. The moment the two words fell out of his mouth, Nelson knew that had to be the name.

It brought together the reason they'd moved and the area's beauty.

"Hey, man, what are you doing down here?" Maverick asked as he strolled down the wood planks.

Maverick was two years younger. He'd chosen to leave the military six months before Nelson, but for different reasons. He'd fallen madly in love and wanted to settle into family life. Unfortunately, she didn't want to move to Lake George and open a family business, which was the end of Maverick's love life.

Or at least the kind of romantic entanglement that required Maverick to be considered a taken man.

Currently, he played the field, not wanting to go down that road again so quickly.

Nelson honestly didn't feel too horrible about his brother's breakup because Maverick's ex was a bit of a bitch. Neither did their other brother, Phoenix. In the end, this is what had been best.

For all of them.

They were more than best friends and brothers. They had a unique bond that couldn't be broken. Whoever came into their lives needed to understand and be willing to accept their special relationship.

Or talk a walk.

"Taking a breather," Nelson said.

"It looks more like you're avoiding the party of four recently seated in the main dining room." Maverick arched a brow.

Nelson sipped his coffee. His brother wasn't wrong. Seeing Marcus, Chuck, Josh, and Tyler again only served to remind Nelson of why he'd left Delta Force. Nelson had a hard time believing that the four had randomly shown up at his restaurant. He didn't believe in coincidences. Marcus and Tyler were originally from the West Coast. Chuck grew up somewhere in Colorado, and Tyler was from Minnesota. Upstate New York was a long way from home for any of these men.

Last he heard, they were all still active duty, stationed at Ft. Bragg, but that could have changed in the previous year. Nelson didn't make a habit of checking up on them. He'd hoped he would never have to see them again.

"What happened on that mission wasn't your fault," Maverick said, holding up his hand. "You did everything you could. Your judgment was not clouded because you knew Roxy's husband was on that SEAL team."

"Doesn't matter. She lost her husband and then her baby; it was my fault. Something she and her asshole brother will never let me forget." Not that he could ever let it go anyway. It had been some time since Nelson had this discussion with anyone, including his brothers. While it haunted his mind daily, he didn't like being reminded of it outside of his memories. He'd been responsible for his team and the rescue of a Navy SEAL team.

And he had failed miserably.

While he was given an honorable discharge from the military and a couple of medals, his parents still thought he was crazy for leaving when he did, especially his father who happened to be a general in the Army. Both his parents believe it tainted his record to leave on such a low.

But he had nothing left.

"You're not the only one who has lost men while serving." Maverick folded his arms and widened his stance. "And Roxy isn't the first widow."

"You know Seth's death and her losing the baby wasn't the only thing that happened." He downed the rest of his beverage, wishing he'd made it an Irish coffee. "I'm done with this topic. I'm doing my best to move on."

"She lied to you, and you made a mistake. You were lonely." Maverick shook his head. "You've never fully dealt with what happened and I'm sure seeing those yahoos—especially Marcus—is bringing it all to the forefront."

Nelson knew his brother meant well, but it didn't change the fact that Nelson had slept with a married woman. "Time to drop it."

"That's hard when it's staring us in the face." Maverick had been looking for something to do when Nelson decided it was time for a change. He thought nothing of packing up and moving to Lake George to start a business with his brother. Phoenix, however, left the military due to an injury. It wasn't career-ending, but it gave him all the reason he needed to join Nelson and Maverick in the restaurant business.

The three musketeers. One for all and all for one, just like when they'd been kids. They'd always been as thick as thieves. Best friends. There wasn't a time in his life when he didn't enjoy either of his brothers. He never once thought of them as pesky little buggers, even though they were younger.

"You're the one who's giving it breath." Nelson leaned over and rinsed out his mug in the cold water.

Maverick raised his hands. "Why don't you take the day? Phoenix and I can handle things."

"Whatever happened to hiring a better management team so we could spend time hiking, fishing, and other activities?"

"That will happen when we learn not to be such control freaks."

Nelson glanced toward the deck of Blue Moon. A few patrons sat outside, enjoying the sunshine. They had heaters for those who thought it was too cold, but most were locals, and this temperature was considered shorts and T-shirt weather. He'd come to this little piece of paradise because he didn't want to have the constant reminder of the death that had surrounded his last mission. It was bad enough it visited him every time he closed his eyes. He didn't need it during his waking hours. But to run and hide from Marcus and his crew would be cowardice.

He wouldn't do that.

Not today.

"I'll be fine," Nelson said. "Besides, it's not like we're running a hotel. They will eat their meal and leave. No worries."

"Just don't get into it with them, even if they start."

"What makes you think I would? We have a business to run, and I would never do anything to jeopardize what we've started." Nelson held his brother's stare, daring him to push his buttons.

"Because I know you and if they come at you, you're not the kind of man to back down." Maverick held up his hand. "For the record, I wouldn't either and remember, I've got your six, so text me or if I see them chatting you up, I'll come running."

"I definitely shouldn't be alone with them." Nelson strolled up the dock. He'd once let his temper get the better of him and threw a punch at Marcus.

But he deserved it.

However, Nelson knew he needed to keep his emotions in check. It wouldn't bring his team back. Or the SEALs he'd been tasked to rescue.

Maverick squeezed his shoulder as they meandered down the dock. "Brandi's here."

A smile tugged at his lips when a certain female came into view. He hadn't seen as much of Brandi Grant during the winter months, and he hated to admit it, but when she wasn't in the area, or in his bed, he missed her. A lot. But now that her brother's wife had given birth to a precious baby girl a couple of weeks ago, she mentioned she wanted to come up as often as possible to see her niece. As in every weekend.

Today, she was hosting a meeting at Blue Moon with Delaney Burdette, the wife of an ex-New York State trooper who now worked for a local private eye firm. Delaney also happened to be one of Brandi's authors. He'd ensured she had the best table in the house and spotted them a nice bottle of champagne as he knew they were celebrating a new book deal.

The last few times they'd seen each other, Brandi

only had a few hours to spare, and the moment they saw each other, they didn't bother with small talk. They went straight to the bedroom. His physical attraction to her was intense and often overwhelmed his ability to think straight. But he wanted more and this weekend he hoped they could at least spend one full night together. Maybe engage in some light conversation, something they didn't often do. However, he wanted to get to know her better. It was scary territory for him, but it was time to move forward with his life.

They were two ships, sharing an occasionally really good sexual encounter. He liked the freedom that allowed and so did she; however, seeing her again, his heart ached for something a little more intimate.

His mind craved intellectual stimulation.

And his soul desired a connection.

His reality dictated that he'd forever be single. The dark cloud that hung over his head was going to dump a thunderstorm, and it hovered a hundred feet away.

"What's really going on with the two of you?" Maverick asked.

"Nothing serious, that's for sure." Nelson shrugged.

"But it's something."

Nelson didn't feel comfortable discussing his love life with anyone, including his brothers. He considered himself a private man in that department. He hadn't been in a real relationship in ten years, and that one had ended badly. He'd never met a woman who rocked his world so much that he cared to change his ways. He liked sleeping in the middle of the bed. He enjoyed being a selfish man. Doing what he wanted, when he wanted. The idea of bending for someone hadn't been all that appealing.

Last year, when he first met Brandi, she came and went like the rising tides. She'd text him when she was heading up to visit her brother and they'd find a few hours together. The sex was hot. But that's all it was. There were no lingering emotions.

There certainly wasn't any guilt.

Or at least that's what he told himself.

But things had slowed in the winter months, and that bothered him in ways he hadn't expected.

He'd felt alone during the six weeks he hadn't seen her right after the holidays. He didn't like that feeling and seeing her again made him never want to experience the emotions he'd been avoiding. The thoughts he'd been entertaining about having one exclusive person in his life were unwelcome, and yet he couldn't rid himself of them.

Each time she showed up, it became harder to ignore the grip she had on his heart.

"She's nice and when she comes to visit, I like hanging out with her, but I can take her or leave her," Nelson said. However, that wasn't true and no one else turned his head. Not that he was looking. Women complicated life and at his age, that was the last thing he needed.

They hadn't defined what they were, so they both could see whomever they wanted, and he was fine if she had someone down in New York City. Nelson hadn't been looking for commitment.

As crass as it sounded, he thought all he wanted was a warm body and kind soul to spend a little time with when it tickled his fancy.

That's what he kept telling himself over the last few months as she slowly came back into his life.

He couldn't live with that lie anymore, but he wasn't exactly sure what he wanted either.

"Then why are you so miserable when she's not here?" Maverick asked.

"That's a stretch."

"It's the truth." Maverick stepped up onto the deck of Blue Moon. "And you deserve a little happiness in your life, so why not make it real?"

Nelson laughed. "I can rattle off a dozen reasons. The first one is we live four hours apart, but the most important one is neither one of us wants anything other than a good time." He handed his mug to one of the waitstaff as they passed by. "Now, I'm going to do my best to avoid Larry, Moe, Curly, and Dumbass by going up to the office. If anyone needs me, send them up there."

"You mean if a sexy redhead with wavy shoulder-length hair asks."

Nelson didn't bother with even a sarcastic remark. He waved his hand over his head and strolled toward the kitchen and the staircase that led upstairs. He pushed open the office door where he planned on remaining until Tyler, Marcus, Chuck, and Josh left.

He sat behind the big desk and pulled out his cell.

Nelson: *Hey. Saw you walk in with Delaney. If you have time after your meeting, text me. I'm up in the office.*

Bubbles appeared.

Brandi: *Does it have a lock?*

God, he wished.

Nelson: *Nope.*

He and his brothers generally hung out together either at the restaurant, at one of their homes, or went camping, though never all three of them. Right now, at least one needed to be at Blue Moon. Occasionally, they hung out with some of the locals. They'd become friends with some of the troopers. Blue Moon hosted a few of their parties and they went out of their way to donate to the local office and the Lake George Patrol.

Brandi: *Too bad.*

Nelson: *We still on for tonight?*

Brandi: *I have another meeting with a potential new author right after this one, and then dinner with my brother and his family. The earliest I can get away is eight.*

Nelson: *Eight it is.*

A tap at the door startled him and he glanced up.

"Sorry to bother you, boss, but four men are asking to see you," one of his waitstaff said.

"Send Maverick." Nelson rubbed the back of his neck. If Marcus wanted a confrontation, he wasn't going to get it. Not today.

"They requested you."

Shit. "All right. I'll be right down." He quickly shot off a text to Maverick, letting him know he was being summoned. It would be rude as the owner to ignore the guests. It didn't matter who they were or the history involved.

And as Marcus liked to remind Nelson every time they crossed paths, Nelson owed him his life.

It wasn't an untrue statement.

He wanted to take his time, but he knew better than to keep Marcus and his crew waiting. Besides, Nelson wanted to get this over with. He made his way down the stairs, through the kitchen, and into the main bar area where Brandi was the first thing his eyes landed on.

Her wavy red hair bounced over her shoulders. When their gazes locked, she smiled and waved.

He nodded, returning the gesture as he strolled toward Marcus, his mood suddenly cooled. The memories of two years ago filled his mind, heart, and soul like the black plague. "Hello, Marcus," he managed to choke out. The name left a bitter taste on his tongue. No amount of mouthwash would be able to erase that flavor. "Josh, Chuck, and Tyler. Welcome to Blue Moon. I hope you enjoyed your meal. I told your server that it's on the house."

Tyler arched a brow. "That's mighty big of you."

"Considering the last time we ran into each other and the way I behaved, it's the least I can do." Nelson would never apologize for what he did, but he could act as if he had an ounce of remorse.

"Thank you," Marcus said, rubbing his jaw.

"We had no idea this was your place when we walked in." Tyler lifted his beer and took a hearty swig.

Bullshit. Marcus had an ax to grind and if Nelson had been in his shoes two years ago, he would have also wanted answers about his brother-in-law's death; however, he wouldn't have gone about it in such an aggressive manner. He would have gone through proper channels and if he hadn't, he sure as shit wouldn't have spread lies and rumors.

There were so many things that had gone wrong during Operation Moon and in the beginning, Nelson wanted to abort the mission. The weather had been a factor. The intel had been shit. Not to mention the compound where the SEALs were being held captive had more security than originally reported.

But Nelson and his team had a job to do and orders to follow. After making a few adjustments, he was given a directive to go in. He was told there was backup in the area and would be there shortly.

He trusted that information.

Only, Marcus and his team didn't enter the fight until it was too late.

"What brings you to the area?" Nelson decided small talk was the only way he would get through this insanity.

Chuck lifted his hand and wiggled his fingers. "I'm getting married next month so this is somewhat of a bachelor party."

"Congratulations." Nelson braced himself for a missile. This had to be the longest he'd chatted with Marcus and his sister hadn't been brought up. He knew the longer he stood at the table, the more likely that subject would come up.

A fucking goddamned miracle it hadn't already.

"Where's Joe and Tony?" Nelson asked.

"We aren't on the same team anymore," Chuck said.

"I asked them to come, but they had other family obligations." Marcus shrugged. "We're staying at a place called The Heritage Inn. Do you know it?"

Oh yeah. He knew it. It was owned by a man named Reese McGinn and his wife Patty. Reese was an ex-Marine before he worked as a state trooper, only to retire and open his boutique hotel and resort. Nelson made a mental note to text Reese. "You'll enjoy it there. The owner is a friend of mine." Nothing like acting like a dog pissing on his territory and enjoying it.

"Good to know," Josh said.

"How long will you be staying in Lake George?" The only reason Nelson wanted to know was so that he could make sure he stayed as far away from anything these four men did. If he continued to run into these assholes, the more likely the past would be brought up, and then finger-pointing would happen, and fists would start flying.

Nelson understood that *his* mission failed, and *he* failed his men. It wasn't the first time. It also wasn't the first time he'd lost good men. In his line of work, these things happened. It didn't make it okay, and it sure as shit didn't make it easy to deal with. He'd seen his fair share of military shrinks. He had no problem opening up to them about his emotional scars—even those that included Roxy. They were real and the only way to move forward in his life, was to deal with his demons.

But this one had destroyed his ability to see past the fire.

"We're here for nine days," Chuck said.

"Well, I hope you enjoy your stay." Nelson decided that was enough. Why tempt fate. He smiled, turned on his heel, and headed back toward the kitchen.

"Hey. Nelson, wait up for a second." Marcus curled his fingers around Nelson's biceps.

He jerked his arm free. As he turned, he mentally prepared for a fight.

Marcus raised his hands and took a step back. "Jesus, man. You're still as jumpy as ever."

Nelson relaxed his stance. "You should know better than to come up behind me like that. I wouldn't do that to you. Not with our history."

"Fair enough," Marcus said. "Look. I just thought maybe you might want to join us for dinner. Or maybe fishing. I'd like nothing more than to put all that bullshit behind us."

No fucking way. Marcus didn't want to invite him to hang out like nothing had ever happened. He had an agenda. Marcus had point-blank called Nelson incompetent and ripped him a new asshole in front of a review board. He'd even had the balls to suggest that Nelson had put the brakes on Marcus' team coming in.

That didn't happen.

But it had been the *baby killer* comment that still stuck out in his mind, only because Roxy had agreed. She always took her brother's side. Blind loyalty.

She burned Nelson in the worst way. He could forgive her for what she'd done, but he'd never forget.

"I appreciate the offer. I'm even willing to put it behind us and forget about it. But we're not each other's people and we both know it."

"I'm extending an olive branch. I wish you would accept it."

"I bought you lunch. You're welcome in my establishment anytime." Every muscle in his body tensed.

"But I'm swamped here, and you and I have always been oil and water. The past always rears its ugly head. It's not a good idea. Enjoy your time with your buddies."

"I'm really surprised you haven't asked about my sister and how she's doing."

Well, fuck. There it was. Nelson sucked in a deep breath. "Are you itching for a fight?"

"Two years is a long time," Marcus said with a somber tone. "We were both hurting. Seth was one of my closest friends and my sister's husband. It's safe to say none of us were thinking clearly."

Shit. The last thing Nelson wanted to do was stand in the middle of his own restaurant and revisit the past. He could barely do that with the two people who mattered most in his life, so why the hell would he do that with the man who had helped destroy his career, even if Marcus had saved his life.

"But we both failed to see that you lost something too that day," Marcus said. "We were both so stricken with grief that we couldn't see past our own noses. I know I said a lot of shit that I shouldn't have and I'm sorry. I know Roxy is too." He smiled. "She's seeing someone. A doctor. It's serious and I wouldn't be surprised if they get married soon."

"I've only ever wanted her to be happy." Nelson felt as though he'd entered some alternate universe because Marcus didn't apologize to anyone. He was an arrogant prick who thought his shit didn't stink.

This was a setup for something, only Nelson didn't know what.

"If you change your mind about hanging out, here's my number." He held out a card, glancing over his shoulder. "I've got to run. I've got a business meeting with my editor."

"Editor?" Nelson's heart dropped to his toes like a brick hitting the pavement. "What do you need an editor for?"

"My second career." Marcus smiled like a big kid. "I left the military six months ago when I got married." He raised his hand and pointed to a wedding ring.

"Wow. I never thought I'd see the day you'd walk away from the Army."

"Neither did I, but when I got the book deal, it was a dream come true. I've always wanted to be a novelist. Besides, Sally didn't handle the deployments well and now that she's pregnant, I want to be present."

"You're going to be a father. Shit. A lot has happened in two years." Nelson did his best to be charming. He plastered a fake smile on his face. A sliver a guilt filled his heart. He wasn't a cold man. He should be happy for anyone who was in the midst of starting a family. However, there was something fundamentally untrustworthy about Marcus. Everything he did was to serve himself. But who was Nelson to deprive the man of enjoying the kind of happiness a family brought?

People did change, but he didn't believe Marcus was that kind of person.

"Sally has really changed me. She's the one who helped me see that maybe I was little too harsh on you."

"Thanks for that," Nelson said. "So tell me, what's your book about?" He wanted to text Brandi and warn her all about Marcus, but what could he honestly say?

"It's a military thriller."

Nelson swallowed. There were so many rules about men and women in the armed forces writing about their experiences. It would have to be so fictionalized that there was no way anyone could attach his missions to his books. Of course, lots of ex-military wrote novels, so it wasn't impossible. "What publisher?" As if he didn't know.

"Grant Publishing." Marcus jerked his thumb in the direction of Brandi. "I'm hoping to work with them. The woman who is taking the meeting is reading my novel and so far, she's loving it. I'm lucky I mentioned I'd be here. I can't wait to hear what she has to say."

Nelson's stomach soured. There was no way Brandi could have known the history and even if she did, this was a business deal. It had nothing to do with him and everything to do with her making the right decision for her publishing line. "Good luck." He stretched out his arm and shook Marcus' hand.

He watched Marcus saunter back to his buddies while he pulled out his cell and made a beeline for the parking lot. He decided Maverick was right. It was best if he took the day off.

Every time Brandi made it to her brother's house off Cleverdale in Lake George, she wanted to move. The picturesque mountains and the crystal-blue waters called to her in ways New York City hadn't.

And she loved Manhattan.

Or at least she thought she had.

It had been the only thing she'd ever known until Lake had met and fell in love with Tiki. Once Lake had moved, everything in her world changed. She'd been given the one thing she thought she wanted more than anything.

Power in her family's business and the respect from her father that she thought she'd been lacking her entire life.

Only, it fell short.

She wasn't sure if it was wanting a change in scenery, or if it had something to do with Nelson, but there was only one way to find out.

"Where is that adorable little niece of mine?" She barreled through the front door without even ringing the doorbell. Of course, Lake and Tiki had been given the heads-up that she'd left the restaurant and was bringing home their favorite meals.

The sound of a baby wailing in the background led her to the massive kitchen that overlooked Harris Bay.

"Wow. She grew a set of lungs." Brandi left her suitcase in the hallway and set her computer bag and takeout on the counter.

"She's also not sleeping." Lake lifted a bottle of red wine from the cooler. "Would you like a glass?"

"So not fair." Tiki stood in front of the sliding glass door, gently rocking back and forth as she patted a fussy—no, more like angry—Maddie's back. "I could so use an entire bottle."

"You could give up breastfeeding altogether." Lake let out a long breath.

"And let my sisters have one up on me. Not on your life," Tiki said. "It seems my child is the only one suffering from the syndrome known as *let's torture parents all day*."

"That might come from our side of the family." Brandi took the glass her brother offered. She would sip it slowly and possibly not even finish it. She needed to be able to drive to Nelson's, a rendezvous she wasn't going to miss. Not this trip. "My mom couldn't, or wouldn't, breastfeed either of us. She said we were incapable of latching on and all we ever did was scream at her in the process."

"So my husband has mentioned a few times," Tiki said. "I'm going to take her into the master and lie down with her. Hopefully, she'll feed, fall asleep, and we both can take a little nap."

"Sounds like a plan." Lake kissed both baby and mom, in that order. "Holler if you need me."

"You know I will." Tiki scurried off around the corner.

"I'm so tired, but so appreciative of you letting me have six weeks to do not much of anything."

"All I want from you is refuge every weekend, a new book from you in six months, one from the both of you, and one from Tiki in eight, and some help with this military thriller." She reached in her bag and pulled out a manuscript. "I met with the writer. I told him I wasn't done, so I didn't have much advice yet. He's already pitching me on a series, which has merit."

"What's his background?" He sat on one of the barstools and pulled the manuscript in front of him, flipping over the front page.

"A decorated ex-Green Beret. Went to West Point. He left about six months ago when he got married. His wife is five months pregnant. I've only read the first three chapters and it's pretty good. He needs a little coaching and I worry the mission aspect might be a little too real. We'd have to reach out to the military and make sure there's nothing compromising in it."

"That's never fun."

"I've never acquired a book like this before." Brandi had to admit that her new role in the family business was harder than she thought it would be, but her brother had always been willing to lend an ear. "The thing is, this book is really a tragedy. It's got intrigue, mystery, a little romance, but no happily ever after. At least not how he pitched it in his cover letter. When I asked him if there was any truth to the story, he flat-out said absolutely not, although he did say his family dealt with something similar."

"What exactly are we talking about?"

"A soldier dying during a mission and leaving a wife behind. That's the only connection to his personal life. The twists and turns are there was an affair. A baby. A miscarriage. It's an epic story, though I wonder if it wouldn't be better if the heroine didn't lose the child or end up a killer, even though it was in self-defense."

"That's depressing," Lake said. "Who's the father?"

"The way it's written, another soldier, which is who she kills."

"That setup is cliché. It might read better if the husband doesn't die. Is MIA and comes back."

"Perhaps. But the characterization—from what I read—is top-notch."

"So, why am I looking at it?" He folded his arms

over the papers. "You're the senior acquisitions editor now, not me. I work for you."

"That you do." She laughed. "I have my copy on the server." She tapped her bag. "I just want you to read it and give me your honest thoughts. There's something there that's calling me, but at the same time, I have doubts. I want to know if it's because I don't trust I can edit a—"

"Don't sell yourself short. I know you just took over that line and Dad forced your hand in doing so, but you really are the best in the business."

"You're just saying that because you like your nice cushy life, which by the way, I wouldn't mind opening an office here. I mean, you spent a few years working remote. No reason I can't." She arched a brow. "Especially with Edward. Our cousin is killing it. I must admit, I was skeptical when Dad asked me to hire him, but Edward is like a little sponge. He soaks up everything and retains it. I'm totally impressed. I told Dad I want to make him my second. He's considering my proposal."

"That will allow you to take more trips here to visit me—and Nelson."

"What I need is a good second for when Dad actually retires."

"Or maybe Edward will take over so you can live up here full-time and be a remote head of acquisitions editor." He winked. "But until then, you need to spread your little wings and fly."

She rolled her eyes. This wasn't the first time they'd had the conversation, but today she wasn't going to humor her brother. "Promise me you'll read it." She gave him her best *I'll do anything for you* look. "I'm not asking for editorial notes. Just your gut reaction. I want nothing in writing. A conversation next weekend will suffice."

"Fine. Now crack open the food and put Tiki's in the fridge. But I'll eat mine now."

Brandi did as instructed, placing his pasta and meat sauce on a plate. She'd opted for white sauce and shrimp, same as Tiki, only Tiki had chicken instead of seafood. After she'd taken care of all that, she joined her brother, climbing up on a stool. He'd already dived into the manuscript, reading three pages. "Do you want to read or spend an hour with me before I take off for the night?"

He glanced up with both brows arched. "Why? What are your plans? Nelson?"

"It's none of your business."

"Oh, yes it is." Lake waggled his finger. "I know you sneak away to see him when you can. I also know it's been on and off for almost a year."

"Not true," she said. "Ethan and I got back together for a couple of months."

Lake shook his head. "That was a mistake. It's obvious you'd rather be with Nelson, whom I think is a nice guy—"

"I don't need your opinion on who I date."

"I wasn't going to say you shouldn't, so don't go putting words in my mouth." Lake lowered his chin. "What I was going to say was, we don't know him that well because you've been so secretive about seeing him, and then you go off and rekindle something with Ethan. It didn't make sense to me."

"Ethan and I have a long history and I needed to know if there was something there."

"Did you do it because you wanted to or because he came at you with the same old bullshit about how you ended things abruptly and for the wrong reasons?"

"Maybe a little of both. Besides, his parents have always been friendly with Mom and when he came back, they asked us all out to dinner."

"Mom and Dad didn't think Ethan was for you, but they aren't ever going to come out and say that. Not unless they saw that it was getting serious again."

"Maybe they should have," Brandi said. "But it's been over for a couple of months. Ethan is out of my life for good this time."

"So. I ask again. What are you planning on doing tonight?"

"Staying over at Nelson's place."

"I'm glad you can finally admit that to me." Her brother smiled triumphantly. "But now the really tough question. What the hell is going on between the two of you?"

"Sex. Lots of good sex."

Her brother coughed. "Jesus Christ. You're my baby sister. I didn't need to know that."

"You asked." She twirled some pasta around her fork.

He pounded his chest before taking another sip of his wine. "Don't you want more from life? Doesn't he?"

The last year had been a difficult one due to the controversy with Gretchen and how she tried to destroy Lake. Then all the changes in Grant Publishing with Lake giving up his acquiring editor status. He was still an editor and part owner, but he was also a best-selling author and the day-to-day operations fell onto Brandi. Not to mention, her father relied heavily on her, which was fine. She and Lake were begging their father to retire.

So was their mother.

But it would probably be at least another year before that happened.

Brandi had dived into her work with gusto. She loved her job and excelled in her new role. This last year, her fling with Nelson was just what she needed. However, there'd always been a distance between her and Nelson, and she thought that was because neither one of them wanted a lasting relationship. Or at least she didn't want one right at that moment and Nelson maybe never. Although, they never talked about it other than to say neither of them were looking for anything and they agreed not to put a label on it.

When Ethan had come back into her life and reminded her of how she ended the relationship, she felt she owed it to him—and to herself—to see if there was anything there. She'd agreed to give their romance a chance because he did make a valid point. They had a lot of the same interests and for a short time, he gave her everything she needed, except excitement.

And passion.

Not to mention he constantly asked her about what her love life had been like the last year or so. Weirder, he wanted to know who she'd been dating. Like the details. Ethan seemed more interested in what she'd been doing during the time they'd been apart than what their future could be.

One of the many reasons she decided it was time to end it for good.

Nelson had always given her a thrill in the bedroom, but now she wanted more from him, only she wasn't sure Nelson was up for the task. He wasn't an easy man to get to know. As a matter of fact, she knew very little about him, which is what made their rendezvous so exciting. She wanted tonight to be the beginning of something new and special.

"I don't know if he does," she admitted. "When we first got together, it was incredibly casual. I didn't see him at all when I got back together with Ethan. But that didn't last long, and these last couple of months with Nelson have been intense, especially in bed."

"I don't want to hear about your sexual escapades." Lake wiggled a finger in his ear and scrunched his face. "What do the two of you discuss when you're together?"

"Not much. We're busy doing other things." She didn't dare glance up over her plate. "I know he and his brothers all left the military around the same time and decided to go into business together."

"Do you know why?"

"Nope." But she did know something haunted him because the one time she spent the night, he'd been startled awake. That was no big deal, but the fact he'd been covered in sweat clued her in that something troubled him. "And for the record, I might not stay all night, so don't be surprised if I sneak back in at a weird hour."

"Why?"

"He might want me to leave."

"That's weird. He lives alone."

"We're not a couple. At least not yet, and I don't know if he wants things to be exclusive," she said.

"I don't want you driving around in the middle of the night." He shook his head. "And I can't say I'm thrilled with you continuing a casual affair with him if you want more and he doesn't."

"I'd rather you not call it that and for the record, I take the subway sometimes at three in the morning.

Besides, he lives on the opposite side of Assembly Point. It's not that far."

"But it's dark and really, are you going to use coming to see your niece as a booty call all summer?"

She tilted her head. "Seriously? Of course not. But he's here and I deserve to be able to let off some steam and see if there's anything worth pursuing with Nelson."

"All right." Lake nodded. "Let me ask you this. What's the real reason you put things on hold with Nelson?"

"I just told you. I had to know if I'd made a mistake leaving Ethan five years ago." She pushed her plate aside and leaned back. She and her brother had been close their entire lives. She'd been lucky to have a brother she could count on, and vice versa. They'd always been able to be straight with each other, even when they didn't like the words coming out of the other's mouth.

That didn't mean he took her advice. Hell no.

And she often ignored his.

But they heard each other. That was something.

"I could have told you that breaking up with Ethan was one of the smartest things you ever did," Lake said. "It wasn't that I didn't like the man, I did. But he wasn't your type. I'll agree Nelson is more in your lane, but he's a tough read and I wonder if maybe you used Ethan as an excuse because you were afraid to tell Nelson how you really felt."

Her brother wasn't totally wrong in his assessment. "He doesn't talk much. But I need to get to know him better. I sense there's a darkness in his soul and I don't think anyone but his brothers is ever going to be able to touch that."

"We all thought that about Foster. Whatever Nelson's demons are and the fact he keeps them close to the cuff, doesn't mean he's never let anyone in."

"That's different," Brandi said. "Foster's wounds were out in the open. It's not like people didn't know about his ex-wife or the passing of his daughter, especially his current wife. Tonya waited patiently on the sidelines until it was time to help Foster move into the here and now. He needed time to heal, and he needed help to get over his loss."

"It sounds like Nelson could be dealing with something like that based on what you just told me."

"I have no idea." She sighed. Fear prickled her skin. She wanted Nelson to open up and that had been her plan for the evening, but she worried he'd want to skip the small talk and go right to the bedroom, like they always did.

"Are you saying you want to find out?"

"Are you encouraging me to?"

Lake reached across the table. "I want you to be happy."

"I hear a but coming," she said.

"I'm concerned he can't give you what you want, that's all."

"I'm going to talk to him about us and being exclusive."

"I'm glad you're putting you wants and needs on the table. Just be prepared that you might not like his answer."

"Your words are under advisement."

2

Brandi's heart thumped in the center of her throat. Being nervous had never been something she had to deal with on a regular basis. She'd been raised to be confident, even when she wasn't. Hiding insecurities had become an art form for the Grants, something her mother had instilled in both her and her brother.

However, as she raised her finger to the doorbell, all that disappeared, and she was left wondering if she was good enough.

But for what?

A man?

The door rattled and Nelson appeared with a smile. He wore a pair of jeans, a dark button-down shirt, and no shoes.

"Good evening," he said with a sexy drawl and smile. "How's your brother's new baby?"

"Adorable, but not sleeping much."

"That's rough." He stepped aside. His home wasn't near as grand as her brother's house. It was a two-story with four bedrooms upstairs, an eat-in kitchen, a family room, a den on the main floor with a master bedroom suite, and the lower level had a game room. It had obviously been decorated by a man with dark tones and dark leather furniture. But it was still nice. "I can't imagine what that would be like as none of my brothers or myself have ever had kids."

"Last weekend when I was here, Maddie was sleeping for what seemed like an eternity, but now, she screams bloody hell for hours."

"You're welcome to sleep here if you'd like."

If her talk had gone well, that had always been the plan. She held up an oversized bag. "I'm glad you said that because I packed my toothbrush." Hopefully, she wouldn't be leaving in the next hour, because she really wanted things to change between them.

He laughed, taking her bag into his hands. "Can I get you a drink?" He left her duffel on the steps and took her hand, tugging her into the kitchen where he'd set out a tray of cheese and crackers and had a bottle of red already opened and decanted. That was different. Normally, he'd tug her right into the master. "Why don't we sit outside for a little? We don't get many nights like this in April."

While the passion for him still filled her bloodstream, this felt more like a date. She both liked that sensation and found it utterly horrifying. "Sounds good to me." She took the tray of food while he took the wine and two glasses. Stepping out onto the patio, she inhaled the cool evening air. It smelled like a crisp pear mixed with a splash of morning dew. "I love it up here."

"You should get a place of your own."

"If it were that simple." It wasn't like she couldn't afford it. That wasn't the problem. After setting the food on a small table between two chaise lounges, she eased into one of the chairs and stared at the stars and the moon. "I've thought about it, but things are complicated with my dad." This was the first time since she'd known Nelson that they had dove into anything other than the food menu at the restaurant. A good book recommendation. A favorite movie or television show.

But only after they'd jumped into bed and were getting dressed before she dashed out the door.

This was a good start to getting to know him better and she wasn't going to ruin it by doing what she always did and use sex to avoid what she really wanted.

Nelson handed her a very generous pour. He pulled his chair closer and stretched out his legs. "You've never talked much about your dad. Or your famous movie star mom."

She burst out laughing. "So, you do know my family."

"Your mother is an amazing actress and she's starring in a role of a lifetime. Kind of hard to miss." He clanked his glass against hers and smiled. "But I figured you preferred to keep that private. I'm sure having an actress for a mom has had its ups and downs."

"Oh. It sure has." She loaded a cracker with a large piece of cheese and slice of pepperoni. "My dad hasn't made it any easier. Being a Grant and owning a publishing company has had its share of challenges too. I don't know what's worse. People asking me weird questions about my mother or slipping me manuscripts under the bathroom stall."

"I think I'd prefer to be shot at."

She scowled. "That's not funny because I've seen the scars on your body."

He reached out and curled his fingers around her forearm. "I don't mean to belittle my wounds. But you must understand that I have to be able to make light of some of the things that happened to me on the battlefield, or I'd go crazy."

"May I ask you something personal?"

"Sure, but be prepared I might not want to answer."

Well, that was honest. She shifted sideways, bending her knees. This was not the first thing she'd thought she'd be asking, but he'd opened the door. "A while back, when I spent the night, you had a bad dream." She had chosen not to ask him about it then because she'd already decided to go back to the city and give Ethan a second chance. When that ended, and she returned to Lake George and her fling with Nelson, it never happened again, and she didn't feel comfortable bringing it up.

But now she wanted to know something intimate about him and this was a good place to start.

"I did?" He turned his head, lifting his wineglass to his lips, and sipped. He kept his focus on something in the distance. "I don't remember."

"You woke up all sweaty."

He shrugged. "I'm sure it was nothing."

"I don't believe that." Placing her hand on his thigh, she squeezed. "Your whole body was shaking. Something obviously spooked you."

Turning his head, he caught her gaze with an intense stare. His blue eyes tore right through her soul, sucking the life out of her. "I'll fill you in on my nightmare if you answer me something."

"Okay." She swallowed. It was only fair that she be open to share intimate details of her life.

"Why did you ghost me for about six weeks this winter? And ever since then, you haven't been around much."

She blew out a puff of air. If she lied, it would be a lot easier to go about spending the night. But then if he found out, getting to know him better would most likely end.

However, being truthful might do the same.

"Something happened that put me in a weird situation."

"What does that mean?"

"Right after the New Year, my ex-boyfriend moved back to town and to be totally honest, there were a lot of things between us that were left unfinished. I felt as though I needed to give him another chance, but right after Valentine's Day, it ended."

"Oh. So you were in a relationship. That explains a lot of strange text messages."

"I should have told you what was going on." She set her glass down. "I had broken up with Ethan a long time ago. He'd been discharged from the Navy."

"He was a military man?"

"He served for six years, but he wasn't cut out for the lifestyle. Anyway, he was moving across the country and my father kept telling me that Grant Publishing could be run solely by my brother and that I should follow *my man* and *his career*."

"That's uncool."

"That's what I thought, and Lake backed me. But I did care for Ethan, and I've always wondered if I made a mistake. Turns out, breaking up with him had been the right decision."

"Does Ethan agree?"

"It doesn't really matter. It's over and I'm sorry I left you hanging. I needed a little time to think, and then when I came back around to talk to you, well, we kind of just picked up where we left off."

"Not exactly," Nelson said. "You've been different, and I've never understood why."

"I've been meaning to talk to you about all this, but we always end up in bed together."

"I appreciate the honesty and I'm sorry if I've made it seem like that's all I want. I've always enjoyed your company. We do have fun together."

"Yes, we do." Time to test the waters, one foot at a time. "Except all our enjoyment is in one area. Not that I'm complaining, but maybe we could do some other things."

"We could. Do you like hiking? Or fishing?"

"I like the former. I'm not sure about the latter. I've never been."

He chuckled. "We can try it and see what you think."

"I'd like that." She lifted her finger and chewed on her nail. "It's your turn to tell me about your dream."

"I was hoping you'd forget."

"You don't have to tell me if you really don't want to. I'll understand."

He stood and strolled across the deck. Leaning over the railing, he looked out over the water and sipped his wine. "No. We made a deal and being with you like this is nice." He turned, catching her gaze. "My last mission with Delta Force I was tasked with a search and rescue mission of a Navy SEAL team. I failed."

What little she knew of the military came

barreling into her mind. Every book she'd ever read on the subject assaulted her brain. Lake had once edited a book by an author who'd suffered PTSD after months of captivity. He'd been rescued by a JSOC team, but it took years of therapy before he'd been able to recount the story. Even then, he often had to pause to spend some time in therapy so he could continue. It took him three years to finish the book with the help of a ghost writer. It sat on the *New York Times* bestseller list at number one for twenty-eight weeks.

"I don't pretend to understand much about the military, or your job in Delta Force, so may I ask what you mean by failed?" She held up her hand. "I asked because we've done many nonfiction books and sometimes it means good men and women have died and other times it means targets, assets, or intel were not obtained."

"That's a fair question." He swirled his wine, staring at it as if it were going to speak for him. "All the men in the SEAL team died before my men and I could get to them."

She swallowed her breath. "I'm so sorry."

"It gets worse. You see, I was team leader. I was responsible for my men. I was the only one who made it out alive." He set his glass down and lifted his shirt, showing off five scars in his abdomen and a crooked scar that looped from his stomach to his side to his back. "The team that rescued me broke five of my ribs performing CPR in the field to bring me back to life. I was dead for at least four minutes. I'm lucky I don't have brain damage, but I'm not right in the head if you asked my brothers."

"Please don't joke about that." She jumped to her feet and raced to his side, wrapping her arms around his bare middle, tracing her fingers along the jagged skin. "I'd have nightmares if I had died."

"My bad dreams aren't about me, but about all the men who perished because of me." He pushed her away. "It's my fault. I screwed up."

She knew enough about what he suffered to take a step back and not take it personally. She didn't believe for one second that he was negligent. His job required him to do things that often had outcomes that ended with the loss of life. She'd read about it, but never faced it firsthand. "I understand you feel that way."

"Do you?" He glared.

"Yeah. I do," she said with a firm, but kind tone.

"You can't," he said. "You haven't lived it and you don't know what war is like."

Shit. This wasn't her area. She had no one to ask for help on what to say or how to handle Nelson's grief and pain. God, she hoped she was doing the right thing. "You're right. I don't. But what I do believe is that you're a good man and you didn't let anyone die unnecessarily. You did what you thought was the right thing at the time. No one can fault you for that."

"Do you want to know what kills me about that mission?"

"Okay."

"I was awarded the Bronze Star for my actions in that battle, even though every man under my command died. The irony in that is stunning. I didn't—don't—deserve it."

"Sometimes life isn't about bravery and being saved in the moment," Brandi said. "But perhaps whatever you did had a bigger impact."

Nelson nodded. "Enemy intel was intercepted thanks to my efforts and a terrorist attack was stopped. I do sleep a bit easier knowing that innocent lives were saved."

"That has to help put some things in perspective." She knew it didn't make up for lives lost. However, the few military personnel she knew wholeheartedly believed that if they died in the line of duty and it saved even only one innocent life, it would be worth theirs.

"Some days it does; other days it doesn't," he said. "You have to remember, those men were like family to me."

"Is that what your dream was about?"

"It's not about one particular mission, but a compilation of everything I've seen in war."

"There's a name for that." She inched closer, careful not to touch him, even though she so desperately wanted to.

"I'm well aware and before you ask the next question, yes, I've been to therapy." He reached out and tucked a piece of hair behind her ear. His fingers lingered across her neck. "I have triggers. The holidays are one. The anniversary of the mission is another. And running into the men who ended up saving my sorry ass."

She squinted. "I would think they would trigger something else."

He chuckled. "Gratitude is hard to come by when you're the only one left standing."

"Oh, God. That was a horrible thing for me to say. I'm so sorry."

He looped his arm around her waist and drew her close to his chest. Pressing his lips against her cheek, he whispered, "Guilt tends to kick in every time I feel grateful to be alive."

"Do you ever try to consider what your teammates would be doing if the tables were turned?"

"I like how you're not afraid to speak what you think." A broad smile appeared on his face. "That's an exercise my last therapist had me do and it has been helpful because deep down, I would want them to go on with their lives. To be happy and fulfilled. I can't expect it to be different for me."

She palmed his cheek. "But living it has to be hard."

Nelson's heart beat so fast he struggled to hear the crickets chirping in the background. His emotions had been swirling in his gut all day. He'd tried going for run. Lifting weights. He did everything he'd been taught to deal with his demons.

But they wouldn't go away. They festered in the back of his mind every damn day. However, he'd managed to carve out a decent life for himself. His restaurant was doing well, and he had his brothers at his side.

What more could he ask for?

He curled his fingers around her wrist and lowered her hand. Her green-blue eyes were warm and caring. It had been a long time since he felt safe in a woman's embrace.

If ever.

But especially since what Roxy had done. That level of betrayal to both her husband and to Nelson felt diabolical. Outside of his two brothers, the only human he'd ever told what really happened had been his therapist. Roxy's family had their version of the truth and Nelson didn't bother to correct them. They slung their mud in his direction but ultimately kept it quiet. They didn't want Seth's good reputation to be tainted by an affair, even though it would have done more damage to Nelson.

He didn't know why they chose to keep the one-night stand quiet, but he often wondered if that dirty little secret would come back and bite him in the ass.

"Sometimes I feel as though I'm barely existing. It goes from one trigger moment to the next, hoping something will change."

"Did something happen?"

He let out a long breath. "I've been selfishly using you. Asking you to spend the night—"

She covered his mouth. "You can't use someone unless they expect something other than what you're offering."

"What if I want to change the dynamic of what's happening between us?" This wasn't the best direction to take the conversation. It wasn't so much that he wanted a long-term, serious relationship with Brandi, but he wanted more than sex.

He'd wanted to be grounded. That's why he'd come to Lake George. He had one foot here and he needed to plant the other one. He wasn't capable of love. He had no idea why, but it had never happened for him, and he figured at his age, it wasn't in the cards. He accepted it, but that didn't mean he didn't want someone in his life.

Intimacy had always been what destroyed his relationships.

Brandi offered him something that could work because there was built-in separation. He could keep her at a safe distance, but still have someone who brought a bit of normalcy.

She arched a brow. "I'm listening."

"This conversation isn't scaring you off?" He

lifted his glass, swirled the red liquid, and sipped, keeping his gaze tightly locked with hers. This was a crazy move. His motives were split. He did want this, but he wanted something else too and if she ever found out, she'd have his head served on a platter.

"Was that your intention?"

"Other than the first night we hooked up, we haven't gotten past hello before ripping each other's clothes off." He waggled his finger between them. "This is the first real conversation we've had and it's pretty intense." He'd started this evening with the thought he'd keep her at arm's length. Marcus had gotten into his head and twisted his emotions. Nelson couldn't think straight. One second he wanted to put his fist through a wall, the next he wanted to drown himself in a bottle of rum. What happened with Roxy had nothing to do with his performance or the outcome of his mission.

But if Marcus was telling the truth, and Seth had found out, that SEAL team's fate could have been a different story.

The problem with Nelson playing this tape repeatedly in his head was that he had no idea what version of the truth Seth had uncovered before he died, because Roxy's was total bullshit.

"What are you suggesting?" she asked.

"I honestly don't know. We've always said this was a fling. No strings. No exclusivity, and to be fair, I still don't see myself as a man who could be in a permanent relationship. I wasn't even sure I would bring any of this up tonight because of how confused I am."

"Why did you?"

That was a valid question and a million answers floated through his mind. He did want to get to know her better. He certainly had feelings for her. Both of those things were true. If he were a different man, he'd jump into the deep end, but he couldn't bring himself to do it. This wouldn't last forever. He couldn't give her everything she deserved, but it could be something great in the moment.

He also needed to know what the hell Marcus was writing about, and he wasn't going to ask the devil. He blew out a puff of air. He wasn't sure if she'd seen him conversing with Marcus or not. Or if Marcus had informed her that they knew each other. She hadn't mentioned it, so he wanted to assume she was in the dark.

However, assumptions were dangerous.

"I picked up my cell at least a dozen times to cancel," he admitted.

"Why?"

"Two reasons." He raked a hand across the top of his head. "The first one was based in fear because things feel different, and I wasn't sure if that was me or you. I don't do relationships and to be fair, I'm not sure you and I are a good idea because I don't know what you want." He held up his hand. "But the bigger reason is I heard from someone in my past. It stirred up a lot of things. Stronger than over the holidays when I had that bad dream. But each time I held my phone in my hands, I couldn't bring myself to tell you not to come. My therapist was always telling me I needed to talk with someone other than my brothers about what happened. I guess that's what I'm doing." He smiled weakly. "I'm sorry for using you in a different way."

She poked his arm. "How can you be using me when we were just discussing dating?"

"Is that what we were doing?" He took her chin with his thumb and forefinger. "I do really like you. I don't want to hurt you and I fear I'll do that in the end."

Her plump lips parted. "Because you don't want the happily ever after?"

He chuckled. "I've never lasted more than a year with anyone since I was in my twenties. It's not fair of me to ask you to give me a chance when I'm telling you that I've never considered marriage or family."

"Those two things haven't been on my radar most of my adult life, but it is something I'd like in the future." She cocked her head. "Are you saying it's completely out of the question?"

A couple of years ago, he would have told her under no circumstance would he even entertain the thought. Now, he wasn't so sure. "I honestly don't know." He pressed his finger over her lips. "It's not fair to ask you to stay involved with me if that's what you really want."

"I came here tonight to talk to you about making this more official." She smiled. "Right now, all I want is to get to know you better and for this to be exclusive. I don't know what the future holds. No one does, but for right now, this is what I want."

"Are we going to have a long-distance romance?" He kissed her sweet mouth. The second their tongues twisted and rolled around each other, all his reservations about being with her melted away like a piece of ice in the hot sun on a summer day.

She patted his chest. "I have a confession to make."

"What's that?"

"I want to take advantage of you and finish this conversation over waffles."

He laced his fingers through hers and tugged her across the patio and toward the first-floor master. "I prefer pancakes." As soon as he closed the sliding glass door, he pressed her against the wall, shoving his knee between her legs. He fumbled like a horny teenager with little to no experience with the buttons on her blouse. It took forever to remove her clothing. When they were both finally naked, they tumbled to the bed.

She wrapped her arms and legs around his body. Her skin sizzled under his touch. All her muscles twitched with every kiss. All he wanted to do was feel her quiver with delight. To hear his name roll off her lips while her orgasm tore through her body.

Licking her way down the center of his chest, across his stomach, she took him into her mouth.

He groaned, fisting her hair, doing his best to maintain control, something that had proved impossible with her in the past. Everything about her drove him wild. No other woman he'd ever been with had ever given him the kind of pleasure that she had.

"Hey," he managed. "Up here."

She lifted her gaze, licked her lips, and smiled.

"You're going to be the death of me." He flipped her onto her back and sucked one of her nipples into his mouth. His hands roamed her body, finding every erogenous zone. Bringing her close to the edge, but not over became an art form.

Her back arched and she begged for him to take her, but he continued to tease and torture. He kissed and licked and tasted until he couldn't stand it.

He entered her slowly, pushing into her inch by glorious inch. Gritting his teeth, he kept things slow and tender. In the past, sex with Brandi had always been wild and out of control. There had never been a lack of passion between them and that hadn't changed. However, holding her in his arms tonight, this felt more like an attachment.

That should scare him enough to make him want to run.

He'd come to Lake George to learn how to keep

his past where it belonged. He understood the move had been more about hiding from it than accepting it. He believed the longer he lived away from having the triggers of the past in front of his face, the more likely they wouldn't affect his daily life.

That hadn't been true so far.

But being with Brandi—opening to her—a few pounds lifted off his shoulders.

He dabbled kisses on her neck and nibbled on her ear.

Her heels dug into the back of his knees, and she dragged her fingernails across his shoulders. Her hips rolled against his, encouraging him to go faster, harder.

Rolling over to his back, he gripped her hips. Their eyes locked gazes and everything he'd ever worried about in life got lost in her sweet blue-green orbs. His breath caught in the center of his chest.

"Yes, Nelson," she whispered as her body convulsed. Her orgasm coated him like the sun's rays reaching down from the sky and spreading across the lake.

His climax exploded, slamming into her like fireworks.

She collapsed on top of him with a big sigh, kissing the center of his chest.

Running his fingers up and down her spine, he stared at the ceiling fan as it slowly turned in the moonlight filtering through the sliding glass doors.

This had become home. A place he could put down his own personal roots. His two feet. Having been in the military, home wasn't something he ever thought about. It was a distant concept that he never thought he needed. He went wherever his CO told him to. Wherever the mission demanded.

Brandi rolled to her side, dropping her arm and leg over his body.

He pulled the covers up and kissed her forehead.

Last weekend, she was already out of his bed and getting dressed by now. Other than that one night, one of them always made the decision that long awkward pauses after sex would never happen.

Lifting her chin, he kissed her sweet lips.

She rested her head on his shoulder and chuckled. "Are we really going to try this long-distance thing?"

There was no doubt he liked Brandi. More than any girl he'd met in a long time. And hell, he'd been the one to bring all this up, but he'd had an ulterior motive.

The damn fucking book.

"I want to but are you sure you do, considering all that I told you about not being a long-haul man?"

She palmed his cheek. "All I ask is that you don't see anyone else and that you're honest with me. If something changes and you want this to end or you find that you're interested in someone else, you need to tell me."

"That works in reverse." He arched a brow. "You can't disappear on me again."

"Point taken."

"I guess I got myself a girlfriend." His brothers were going to have a field day with this one.

And Marcus was going to have something to say about it too when he found out, especially because Nelson didn't mention it during their conversation.

Well, it wasn't any of Marcus' damn business.

However, now that he and Brandi were official, he needed to decide if he should tell her about his connection to Marcus or not.

"Good night, Brandi," he whispered.

"Sleep well."

3

"Thanks for meeting me so early." Nelson leaned against his Jeep. It was rare he went outside of his family for advice or help. However, in this instance, his brothers had agreed Marcus couldn't be trusted.

"I had to help get the kids up for school. Now that two of them are teenagers and the youngest is eleven, you'd think they'd be able to wake up to an alarm, but I can't tell you how many times Justin has missed the bus." Reese folded his arms across his chest and leaned against the fence between the main hotel and his private home.

"I used to pay Maverick to oversleep so that it would throw off the rhythm and we'd all get a ride. Drove my parents nuts."

"I don't mind driving them, but Patty thinks I'm

too soft when it comes to the kids and she's right." Reese shook his head. "Anyway, I'm glad you reached out. I wanted to thank you for offering all my guests a discount at your restaurant and putting up a sign."

"Anything for a former military man." Nelson nodded. "We appreciate you telling your customers about Blue Moon."

"What is it that I can do for you this morning?"

Nelson had gotten to know most of the men who either worked for Jared Blake or used to work for him at the local New York State Trooper office. They were good people, and Nelson and his brothers always opened their restaurant to whatever they needed. "I'm a little uncomfortable asking you this, but I was hoping you could keep an eye on four of your guests and just let me know if they're up to anything strange."

"Are we talking about Marcus Fumen and his friends?" Reese lowered his chin.

"That's the group."

"I take it you served with them?"

"They're Green Berets. I was Delta Force. But our paths crossed in Ranger School and on a few missions. I also dated Marcus' sister a long time ago." Nelson saw no reason to keep any intel from Reese. Deep down, Nelson knew he could trust the information would be safe. "The relationship ended badly. She wanted more than I could give. Eventually, she moved on and married a SEAL. Long story short, I was on a search and rescue for her husband's team, and I couldn't bring him home. I failed. My entire team died during the mission. It was a fucking disaster."

"Sounds like you still blame yourself."

"It's hard not to. When I ran into Marcus, he gave me this song and dance that he's forgiven me. That it's all in the past, but I don't believe him any more than I believe he had no idea I was living here."

Reese glanced toward the sky. It had started to lighten as the sun approached the top of the mountains. "If he's here for you, what do you think his endgame is?"

"That's the problem. I don't know."

"Is there any chance he's being genuine?" Reese tossed his arm over the wood railing. "Some people do change."

"The venom that he and his sister spewed in my direction was awful. It didn't come from being hurt. Or from grief. I know that kind of anger. I've felt it. I've even expressed it, doing my damnedest to hurt those around me. But theirs came from dark, damaged souls. Not to mention they did everything in their power except expose one secret to try to get the Army to strip me of my benefits and get me dishonorably discharged."

"They addressed the review board of your mission in a negative manner?"

"Oh yeah." Nelson rolled his neck. His muscles twitched and tightened. The names and faces of every single man he lost that day filled his brain. An overwhelming sadness filled his heart, making it difficult for him to take a breath and continue. He took a moment to gather his thoughts. "Marcus made a few bogus claims about how I handled my portion of the mission. Both he and Roxy made up lies about my past with Roxy and painted me to be a vengeful man."

"I've seen the medals hanging in the bar in Blue Moon. I know some of them are yours. That can't be true," Reese said, giving off a vote of confidence and reassurance that he saw through the bullshit and understood the man. Of course, Nelson had heard the stories about Reese's biological father, his first wife, and the tough choices Reese had to make to keep his family safe.

"What they said about my character is totally out of line. How Marcus tried to portray my decisions in a lose-lose situation was absolutely ridiculous and no one believed a word. But the bottom line is good men died and I was responsible for them."

Reese inched closer, rested a hand on Nelson's shoulder, and squeezed. "I know that feeling and it won't ever go away. The intensity will ease, if you allow yourself to move past the guilt."

Nelson felt a sense of camaraderie that had been reserved for his brothers. A piece of the shame he carried lifted. He exhaled. "That's why I moved here. That's what Blue Moon is all about. I'm lucky my brothers have my back. But seeing Marcus brings everything that happened front and center, and I can't shake this feeling that he's up to no good."

Reese ran a hand across the top of his head. "Earlier, you mentioned Roxy and Marcus held back a secret. Care to share what that was?"

Fire filled Nelson's chest. "A couple of months before the mission, Roxy showed up under the pretense that she wanted to see her brother. We were stationed at the same base, only he'd been deployed. That should have been a huge red flag that she hadn't known that juicy piece of information. They are pretty close." Nelson pushed from his Jeep and paced in front of the hood. He hadn't told this story since he resigned from the military and had to explain his reasons to his brothers. There was a fair amount of shame in his actions when it came to Roxy.

However, she'd lied to him and took advantage of his kindness. Of their past.

"She was upset and told me things with her husband weren't good. That they were separated and she was going to file for divorce. That's why she'd come home. I let her in and gave her an ear. Big mistake."

"What happened?" Reese asked.

"I slept with her, and she got pregnant, only, to my

knowledge, she told her husband that the child was his. I hadn't even figured it out until Marcus filled me in after Roxy lost the baby and the math didn't make sense for when Seth had been deployed."

"Jesus. I'm sorry."

"It was a clusterfuck." Nelson paused, lifting his gaze. The tightness in his throat returned. His pulse increased. A vision of death filled his mind. A piercing pain jabbed at his side. He relived the moments of being mortally wounded as if his personal suffering would ease the torture of the loved ones left behind. "I died on that mission, and I don't mean figuratively. I'm standing before you because Marcus broke five of my ribs to bring me back to life. It was his team who joined mine when I called for help. I owe him and he enjoys reminding me of that as much as he got some weird thrill in pouring salt in an open wound."

"You can't make this shit up." Reese pinched the bridge of his nose.

"He had lunch at my restaurant yesterday. He acted as if we needed to put the past behind us," Nelson said. "However, I don't trust Marcus. He vowed revenge. So did his sister."

"If they wanted to bring you down, why didn't they expose your affair? That could have gotten you a less-than-honorable discharge."

"Because it would have tainted Seth's record and it would have hurt Roxy's reputation. She comes from old money and appearances mean everything." Nelson closed his eyes and inhaled sharply. "It's always possible that I wasn't the father, but I'm pretty sure I was."

"Why use you? Considering your history, that's cruel to make you the father."

Nelson blinked. He should have known what Roxy had been up to. Three times that night he'd turned her down. He told her that it wasn't a good idea. She kept telling him they never got to have their goodbye and that she and Seth were done.

It had all been a lie.

"I have no idea what she told Seth, or if he even knew she was pregnant. A long time ago, I cared deeply for her and she for me. But Marcus always got in the way. His jealousy of the way my career turned out tainted mine and Roxy's relationship to the point he poisoned her against me. I don't know what game she was playing. I honestly don't want to know." Nelson sighed. He couldn't believe he was having to deal with this again. When he packed up his life and moved to Lake George, he honestly believed that part of his life was over. "But there is no way in fucking hell Marcus randomly picked the Village of Lake George, and your hotel and resort, which is a stone's throw away from my business, by chance."

"I'll keep my eyes and ears open, but can I make a suggestion?"

"Of course."

"Have you met Katie Donovan and Jackson Armstrong?"

"The private investigators? Yeah. They've both come in with their respective families. Why?" Nelson narrowed his stare.

"Patty and I can only do so much spying. We've got three kids and other guests to deal with. I'm happy to report everything that I see and hear, but Marcus and his buddies don't know anyone here and Katie and Jackson's network is vast. They could plant someone here, using the cabin I keep for troopers or family, giving you more access to what Marcus might be up to."

"I like that idea."

"I'll hook you up with their private numbers. I'm sure they can make something happen today."

"Thanks, man." Nelson stretched out his arm. "I owe you one."

"Anytime." Reese turned on his heel and headed toward the main house.

Nelson climbed behind the steering wheel and quickly shot a text to his brothers that they had a set of eyes at the hotel and might have two. He hit the start button and turned his vehicle around. As he pulled out onto the main road, some of his problems melted away knowing he was headed back to his home and a beautiful, sweet woman waited for him in his bed.

It was an unexpected emotion. Caring for Brandi

this deeply had come out of left field. Enjoying it had shocked his system.

He'd decided to roll with it because this was his new beginning. The clear blue sky that Lake George offered helped open his soul to heal.

All he had to do was get through the next eight days.

Brandi lifted her legs and dropped her feet on the ottoman. Raising the coffee mug to her lips, she took a long slow sip of the bitter brew as she watched the sun lift over the mountains. The sky turned a fiery orange-red. She never saw a sunrise like this in Manhattan. Not unless she was on the ferry, and even then, it was ruined by the tall buildings and lack of lush greenery.

Sucking in a deep breath, she took a moment to enjoy the peacefulness of it all. The hum of a few engines cruising across the lake to find the perfect fishing spot tickled her ears. The birds chirping in the background were the perfect morning music to get her blood pumping.

And all the glorious scents of the crisp lake floating across the air, blooming flowers, and the dew made her never want to leave.

When her eyes blinked open, she'd been surprised to be alone in Nelson's bed. She found a note stating he had an errand to run. That was over an hour ago.

What the hell did he have to do at the crack of dawn? Perhaps he had a meeting with one of his brothers or something. Or a delivery at the restaurant. She had no idea, and she wasn't going to start this relationship off with doubt. Or badgering about where he went off to. She had no reason to be insecure.

Nelson had never been anything but kind and honest. To question him now would be the kiss of death.

She set her mug on the end table and opened her laptop. Even though it was the weekend, she still had to work. In the past, she never cared. She'd spent the last five years or so trying to prove to her father she had what it took to run the business just as well as Lake. That meant long hours and she'd sacrificed any resemblance of a real love life.

It was time for that to change.

Only, now she was taking over much of the daily operations and her workload was greater; therefore, she still had to bring work home.

She logged into the secure server, something they'd made even more difficult for outsiders to hack into thanks to last year's scandal. She pulled up Marcus' novel. Something about this story gave her goosebumps. In a good way. She wanted to flip through the pages like it was candy. The characters jumped off the page. She could relate to them on so many levels.

But there was an underlying tone to it that made her shiver. The tone was too dark, but that could be adjusted.

The story was broken down into three parts, all written in an omniscient point of view. For the most part, the author handled this voice well, although Marcus tended to pull the camera lens too close to third person, making it too personal for the reader during the darker elements of the story.

The first part dealt with the soldier who died and his relationship with his wife and the soldier she had an affair with. She'd only read the opening, but it showed a vibrant woman who loved her husband passionately. This couple had an amazing relationship, but there was a third person who constantly circled their marriage.

A man from her past who continually showed up when they least expected it.

This premise was a little cliché, but she was invested enough in the writing to see where it went.

That didn't mean she'd buy the manuscript.

The second portion covered the details of the mission. How it failed and why the husband died. She had to admit, the failed op reminded her a little about Nelson's story, but many soldiers died during war. And this had to do with how the brother of the wife blamed the man she had a brief affair with.

The man from her past.

That could really be an interesting twist.

The final section centered around the wife, her grief, and her plan for revenge for what she believed was the ultimate betrayal.

It was a little too brutal.

Brandi had no idea if Marcus had been able to pull all the elements together and she worried the ending would be too depressing. Marcus had mentioned that the friend—Willie—was murdered. Brandi wasn't sure about that ending and she let Marcus know that. He had responded that he'd be open to alternate endings but wanted her to read the entire story before she made any rash decisions.

If the story hadn't been so intriguing, she would have written the rejection letter right there. Authors who thought their brilliance happened when they wrapped it all up made her want to pull her eyelashes out one by one.

But her father, and her brother, had taught her that writers could be an interesting group and first-time authors especially proved to be difficult when it came to taking editorial direction.

They needed to be delicately led into doing the right thing.

First, she needed to decide if this book was right for Grant Publishing. Then if Marcus was worth the effort.

Finding where she left off, she began reading. She

pulled out her notebook and pen and began writing down her questions and comments.

This would be one hell of a revise and resubmit letter. And right there, she'd made the decision. Marcus would have to prove he could do the work. If not, no deal. And she wanted to see him work a series. She didn't want a one-hit wonder. She'd done enough of those in her career.

The sound of the sliding glass door opening startled her. She jerked, glancing over her shoulder. "Shit, you scared me."

"Sorry." Nelson handed her a bag from the local pastry store.

"What's this?" She peeked inside the bag. "Oh my God. You remembered chocolate croissants are my favorite."

He tapped his temple. "I remember a lot of things." He strolled across the patio. The scents of pine and soap filled her nostrils. His hair was damp from his shower. He wore a crisp white T-shirt, a pair of jeans, and no shoes.

The man had the sexiest toes she'd ever seen.

"I didn't even hear you come home, much less jump in the shower." She closed her pad and put her computer aside. Pulling out the warm breakfast treat, she broke off a piece and plopped it into her mouth. The milk chocolate melted on her tongue.

It was a little piece of heaven.

"I didn't want to disturb you." He leaned against

the railing across from her, sipping from a travel mug. "You looked hyperfocused, and I didn't want to bother you."

"Aw, that's supersweet."

"I have my moments." He winked. "What are you working on?"

"Reading a submission from a potential new author."

He raised his mug and took a long sip. "Is it good?"

"It caught my attention enough that I want to read the entire thing, but I don't know how much work it needs yet."

"I'm curious. How does that work?" He set his mug on the railing and pressed both hands on the wood. His biceps contracted. "This person wrote a book and now you're going to tell him or her they have to change it?"

It was hard to concentrate on anything when she had a beautiful sunrise, a dazzling lake, and a hot man to grace her vision.

"A good editor's job is to make an author's idea even better. To make the execution of the words literally jump off the page." It was rare she enjoyed discussing her career outside of the office. But with Nelson, it got her blood pumping. "I've never bought a novel that didn't need a little massaging. Some need more work than others. Even seasoned authors run off the rails sometimes and it's my job to bring them back in."

"So, do you think you're going to buy this manuscript?"

"I don't know yet." She polished off the croissant and reached for her coffee. The sun hit her face with the full force of the morning. She'd promised Lake and Tiki she'd be back by lunch to watch Maddie so her brother and his wife could both spend a little time organizing their thoughts for their next book.

"What's it about?"

"I can't tell you."

"Why not?" he asked.

"It would be breaking a confidence." She polished off her coffee and stood. "Writers are a paranoid group and considering some of the scandals that have surrounded my family's company over the years, we've made it a policy never to discuss any author's book until after we've set it out into the world."

"I don't know anything about publishing. Or what it takes to write a book."

She laughed. "I understand all the ins and outs of my profession, except I could never put words on the page. I know what's required to make a bestseller, but I couldn't do it."

"I don't believe that. You're smart. This is your business. I'm sure you could do it with your eyes closed."

"I don't have the patience to sit in a room all by

myself and write about people who don't exist. I don't want to make up conflict. I have a hard enough time dealing with conflict in my own life. I understand how a novel is supposed to be constructed, but doing it myself is just not something I have any interest in doing."

"Did your brother always want to be a writer?"

She nodded. "He's really good too, but he's also an excellent editor. That's a rarity." Brandi tucked her hair behind her ears. Her heart thumped in her throat as she inched closer. Long-distance relationships usually ended in heartbreak. She was flirting with the devil. It would be a long time before her father retired and let her move out of the city.

Her mother would have a meltdown. She already got teary-eyed every single time they all had dinner together and Lake wasn't present. Her parents had come last weekend and would be coming next weekend, but they had to be careful. Her mother just wrapped shooting *A Girl Named Lilly*. Phoebe Grant was currently one of the hottest mature actresses in the entertainment industry and everyone wanted to get a picture and an interview.

"And is running your family's publishing company what you want?" He wrapped his arms around her waist and heaved her to his chest. "Has that been your dream?"

"Actually, it's all I've been able to think about since I was a teenager, but I was always told I'd never get the opportunity. My dad kind of lives in the dark ages."

Nelson kissed the sensitive spot under her ear.

A warm shiver rolled across her skin from her neck to her toes.

"I don't have any sisters and my dad always encouraged my mother's career, so I can't imagine what that was like." He continued to press his hot lips on her exposed skin.

Her muscles twitched under his touch. She could barely think straight, much less form a coherent string of words. She threaded her fingers through his thick hair. "It's not easy," she managed. "Especially when I want to make changes and he fights me every step of the way."

"Does Lake back you?" Nelson's voice rolled across her ears like melting butter on sweet corn. His tongue licked a path down the center of her chest. Taking her shirt between his teeth, he tugged it over her breast, leaving her bra exposed.

She gasped. "He does."

"Does your dad listen to him?" He put his hand inside the flimsy article and found her nipple. He stared into her eyes with an intense, but loving gaze.

"Sometimes," she whispered. "It's really hard to carry on a conversation when you're doing that."

He smiled. "Keep pushing. You'll get everything you want. I'm sure of it."

"Right now, I want you."

Lifting her over his shoulder, he carried her toward the sliding doors to the master.

"What the hell are you doing?"

"You expressed a need; I'm simply making sure it's met." He tossed her on the bed and lifted his shirt over his head. "What are you waiting for? Get naked."

She bit down on her lower lip and watched as he rolled his jeans over his hips. Quickly, she unhooked her bra and wiggled out of the rest of her clothing. She crawled to the end of the bed and ran her hands up his thick thighs, doing her best to ignore all the scars on his body. She knew better than to ask. She'd made that mistake once before and he'd gone quiet.

Silent, actually.

Now that they were an item, he'd begun to open up. It would take time, and she wanted to do this the right way. It was the first time she dated a man whom her parents hadn't somehow had a hand in the setup.

She also wasn't sure if she was going to tell them about Nelson yet, something she'd have to discuss with him—tomorrow.

He pooled her hair on top of her head as she took his length slowly into her mouth.

She'd always been a sexual woman. One of her ex-boyfriends described her as demanding and that had been one of the reasons they called it quits. She found that comical. The sex with him had been a bit on the vanilla side, and that was fine. It wasn't bad; it simply wasn't adventurous.

Nelson was a different breed of man. He enjoyed mixing it up. He could be sweet and romantic in bed. Or he could be wild. And he never had a problem with her taking the lead.

She liked that.

"That's enough of that." He tugged at her hair, then pushed her down to her back, lifting her knees to his shoulders and he lowered his head between her legs. He didn't tease her or give her any warning. His tongue went right for the prize.

"Oh, God." Her chest rose up and down with her raspy breaths. She dropped her head back and tried to focus on anything but the building climax that was going to tear through her system like fireworks. Digging her heels into his shoulders, she raised her hips and rolled with the motion of his mouth, making it harder to savor the moment.

He slipped in two fingers and continued to torture her until her orgasm filled her stomach. Her body jerked and shivered. Her muscles burned from the inside out.

Reaching down, she pushed his head back, needing a reprieve.

He grabbed her by the hips, bent her over the mattress, and thrust himself deep inside. He reached around her waist and continued to rub her hard nub. "Do it again for me."

That simple command sent her body into overdrive. One orgasm after the other spilled from her body.

"Brandi," he whispered in her ear as his climax slammed into hers like a massive wave hitting the breakwall. He collapsed on top of her, gasping for air and holding her tight.

The room spun. She blinked, trying to regain her composure. "Are you going to let me stay over again tonight?"

He chuckled. "Only if we can start the day off right again."

"God, I love morning sex."

"Another thing we have in common." He shifted her body so they were facing each other and kissed her nose.

She laughed. "You like sex, period."

"That's true, but I don't hear any complaints from you." He raised his arm and glanced at his watch. "I hate to do this, but I have to run to the restaurant. We're hosting a private breakfast for some state troopers this morning and I need to be there. Feel free to stay here as long as you need. It's going to be a long day for me, but I should be home between eight and nine. I'll text you the code to the garage."

"Works for me."

He planted a wet kiss on her mouth. "I'll see you later."

She wrapped herself in the sheet and watched

him dress. The relationship part with Nelson might be new, but there was a comfort level with him that came with history. She had no idea what the future held, both with when her father would finally let go of the reins and with Nelson.

But at least she'd taken the risk.

4

"They ate lunch here yesterday. Why the fuck are they back?" Nelson stabbed his salad, but his stomach had soured. He honestly had no appetite, but he needed to eat. He also needed to vent.

His mind had been swirling with images of the past. Ever since he left Brandi at his house this morning, he couldn't focus on anything but all the mistakes he'd made on each mission he'd commanded that failed. The techniques he'd developed to help him get through these moments had been working. He'd been slowly working his way back to the present.

Then Marcus walked through the fucking front door.

"At least we got the heads-up they were coming, and we were able to have a table in a certain area so we can keep a watchful eye on them," Phoenix said.

"He's taunting me." Nelson lifted his water and chugged it down, wishing it were a beer, but he'd wait to have an adult beverage when he got home. His pulse raged. Fuck. It wasn't because a brief thought of Brandi came into his brain. He kept trying to pull up her image—her beautiful smile—instead of all the bad things that happened, but he couldn't let go of the past.

Or maybe the past wouldn't let go of him.

And then there was the fact that he wanted to keep her as close as possible because he needed to know what was in that damn book.

He did care for Brandi, and he did want her in his life. That was all true. He'd been honest about his concern for committing but held back two things.

His knowledge that he knew their relationship wouldn't last. Brandi understood that too. She'd been willing to let him go to give an ex-boyfriend a chance because in the end, she wanted it all. A powerful career and a family.

But she didn't want it in Lake George.

Her life was in New York City.

This was a nice diversion for her, even if she couldn't admit it to herself or to him.

The only problem with this scenario was the fact she was capable of love.

He was not.

"I'm sure he is, but you can't let him get under your skin." Phoenix pushed his empty salad plate aside. "The private investigator—her name is Hensley—is moving into The Heritage Inn as we speak."

"I wish we could have met with her first."

"I agree with Reese. We shouldn't take the risk in talking with her at all. The only time that happens is if she comes into this restaurant, and that won't happen because we'll be in here and she'll be poking around their room or somewhere else."

One of the waitstaff came over with two burgers, a basket of fries, and an order of onion rings. Nelson set up his food and took a bite of his lunch, hoping that would help ease his mind. He made the mistake of glancing over his shoulder. Marcus and his crew had ordered another round.

"Do we know what time their party barge leaves?" Nelson asked.

"I overheard them say four, so they could be here for a while."

Nelson dunked a fry into some ketchup and plopped it into his mouth. "I have to know what he's writing."

"Why?"

"Are you kidding me?" Nelson glared. "I wouldn't be surprised if he's writing about my mission and somehow demonizes me."

"That would be slander and that mission will remain classified for decades. Too many people died. The military will never allow anyone to write about it."

"He could drop it in a different geographical area and change the directive. There are a lot of ways to doctor it up and make it different," Nelson said. "Marcus isn't stupid."

"I'll give you that. However, you realize he not only would have had to research where we relocated, but that you and Brandi are an item. That's a lot of time and energy to put into rattling you. And for what? To publish a book that in the end will have no impact on your life because lies can't hurt you. The Army did their investigation. The case is closed."

Nelson tossed his napkin on top of the plate and leaned back. He hated feeling paranoid. "Are you going to sit there and tell me that you believe Marcus and his friends coming here is a coincidence?"

"I didn't say that." Phoenix was almost four years younger than Nelson, but they were only three school years apart. They were as close as brothers could possibly be. They almost never fought; however, they wore their emotions on their sleeve when it came to each other. They never held back and often gave unsolicited advice.

Usually, it was exactly what the other needed to hear, but that didn't make it any easier to swallow.

"I'm sure he's here to fuck with you and I don't trust that asshole any more than you do. I don't understand why you won't tell Brandi about the history."

Nelson rubbed his chin and glanced out toward

the waterfront. He could have easily done that yesterday, or even this morning. "She's barely my girlfriend and I have no right to run interference with her work. Besides, she hasn't offered him a deal and maybe she won't."

Phoenix shook his head. "You're making a two-folded mistake."

"What does that mean?"

"When Brandi finds out you know Marcus—"

"She leaves tomorrow and won't be back up until next weekend with her parents. She'll be busy with family and she's not ready to say anything to her folks about us, which I'm thrilled about, considering who her mother is."

"I suspect it will be a bit of a media shit show."

Nelson nodded. "I'll be avoiding that at all costs."

"Okay, but if Marcus already knows there's a connection between you and Brandi, what a great weekend to fuck with you." Phoenix arched a brow. "And he can do it in front of cameras."

"That would ruin his book deal."

"Only with Grant Publishing. It might sweeten it for someone else."

"Fuck," Nelson muttered. He hadn't thought about that. "We know Marcus is telling the truth when it comes to when he got married and the fact his wife is pregnant."

"So what? He also minored in English in college," Phoenix said. "He had a collection of short stories published when he was in high school. Him writing a book isn't far-fetched." Phoenix held up his hand. "But I don't believe for one second that he randomly picked Brandi and that's something we have to find out. If you had told her the truth, you could have asked her how it was that he found her. Your second mistake in all of this is pretending that you're not going to care when she dumps your ass for lying to her."

His heart dropped to his toes. "I care that I will have hurt her, but she and I both know this relationship has a beginning, a middle, and an end." No amount of mouthwash would rid the bitter taste that was left swirling around on his tongue. "I've got an idea."

"I'm scared to ask."

"Then don't." Nelson pushed back his chair and stood. He shoved his hands in his pockets and strolled toward Marcus' table. As owners, he and his brothers often went around the room, checking on their guests, making sure the service and the food were up to standard. They were still constantly changing the menu, looking for the right blends. They were close to having it perfect. Their waitstaff and chef were in place.

Their management team was still not where they needed it to be, but they were getting there.

"Good afternoon," Nelson said with his best smile. "I'm glad to see you back. That must mean you're enjoying the atmosphere and the food."

"We asked four different people at the hotel, and we got the same answer. Blue Moon is the best in town." Chuck lifted his beer. "I need to use the restroom."

"I'm right behind you," Josh said.

"Me too." Tyler jumped to his feet.

"Mind if I sit down for a minute?" Nelson waved his hand over one of the chairs.

"Please. Be my guest." Marcus nodded. "Would you like a beer?"

"Thanks, but it's a little too early for me. Besides, I'm working."

"Understood." Marcus lifted his drink and took a long swig, holding Nelson's gaze. "It's beautiful up here. I can see why you and your brothers relocated to the area."

"The winters can be rough." Nelson adjusted the seat to lift his leg and rest his ankle over his knee.

"Is that difficult for business?"

"It's slower than the summers, but the local crowd has been very good to us." Nelson eyed his brother, who had moved closer. Nelson understood Phoenix would be concerned. Marcus and Nelson had never had a conversation that ended well, until yesterday.

That could have been a fluke.

"Would it be okay if I asked you something about your book? I'm curious about a few things," Nelson said. "More so for Maverick than myself."

"Sure. I love talking shop."

Why was Nelson not surprised. "Maverick's always been a huge reader and he's dabbled a little in writing here and there. So, I'm curious as to how you go about getting a book published. Like, how did you find this editor?"

Marcus leaned forward, resting his forearms on the table. "You have to do your research and know what publisher is interested in which type of book. But even more so, which editors in each house are acquiring. I got lucky. I attended a conference that Brandi happened to be speaking at and I was supposed to pitch to her, but because of a scheduling mix-up, she had to leave the conference early. She told the conference coordinators that anyone who had a meeting with her could send a full manuscript. So I did."

"Do editors always set up meetings before they buy books?"

"No." Marcus leaned back. "I hadn't received confirmation that my manuscript landed in her inbox, so I sent another email. I informed her that I was going to be on vacation and would have limited access to communication and asked if she could let me know that she'd gotten it and when I might hear from her. I happened to mention where I was going on vacation, but only because I knew her brother lived here." Marcus shrugged. "I took a chance, and it paid off."

"Smart to do recon like that. Is that why you chose this area?"

Marcus waved his hands. "Oh my, no. That was gravy. We all wanted to go somewhere we've never been. We've been all over the globe and so many different places in the US, but no one had ever been here, except when we all ended up in Fort Drum in the middle of winter. All we saw was snow. Gray skies. And more snow."

"Like I said, it can brutal up here." Nelson chuckled.

"Does your brother really want to write a book?" Marcus held up his beer and lowered his chin.

"It's something he's talked about doing." That wasn't a lie.

Maverick had even sat down with Lake and Tiki once or twice and discussed the process. It wasn't that Nelson didn't believe his brother wasn't capable. It came down to time constraints.

And motivation.

"He's not even close to where he'd have anything worth talking to an editor about, but I thought I'd get some information so I could pass it along to him if he ever chose to pursue it."

"Well, you've got my number. Tell Maverick he can call me anytime."

Nelson tapped his knuckles on the tabletop and stood. "I'll let him know. Thanks for the information." He strolled back into the main room and made his way behind the bar where Maverick had taken over while the bartender took his break.

"I only heard half that conversation." Maverick shook a tumbler and poured it over ice. "But it was the parts that count, and Marcus is gunning for you."

"I know." Nelson snagged a towel and tossed it over his shoulder. Every stool around the bar had been taken. Quickly, he filled two drink orders and took a third. Once he checked on a few other customers, he met his brother in the center. "We have to figure out what he has planned." He lifted his hand, waved, and smiled as Marcus and his crew left the building. "Whatever he's got brewing, it's going to be public."

"You think next weekend?"

"I bet that's only the prologue," Nelson said. "A sample to wet everyone's whistle. He wants to watch me sweat. Well, I'm not going to give that bastard the satisfaction."

5

Brandi set her computer aside, leaned back, and took a long breath.

"That was a big sigh." Her brother strolled into the family room carrying a stack of papers. "What's wrong?" He made himself comfortable on the other side of the sofa.

"New writers who don't understand how traditional publishing works." Handholding had always been a part of an editor's job when it came to a debut author, but it was made easier when that writer had an agent. That's why for the most part, Grant Publishing didn't accept unagented manuscripts.

"Who exactly are we talking about?" Lake kept a finger on the pulse of the business. Not because he and their dad didn't believe she could handle running the company, but for years he'd had her job and the transition had taken some time.

She also sought out his help more often than her father's. Lake gave her the kind of insight she needed without telling her what she should or shouldn't do, whereas her father made demands.

"Marcus Fumen."

"Ah, the author of the insanely good idea, but not executed as well as it could be."

She jerked her head. "You finished it? In two days? With a newborn screaming all night long?"

Lake lowered his chin. "How would you know what my child does all night? You've slept at Nelson's house all weekend."

"Are you telling me that your daughter has suddenly started sleeping more than ten minutes at a time?"

Lake laughed. "She lasts a little longer than that, but unfortunately, I got up with her every single time she woke last night."

"I thought Tiki was breastfeeding and she would let you sleep unless the little cutie pie couldn't go back to sleep."

"The moment Maddie cries, my eyes open. I ended up reading and making notes the last two nights." Lake shrugged. "How far have you gotten?"

"Halfway," she admitted. "And I'm slightly losing interest. The mission is exciting, but the POV (point-of-view) shifts are jarring. I get he's trying to pull the camera back because a lot is happening, but I think this story needs to be tighter. I'm not sure he's telling the right story."

"Your instincts are spot-on, as usual." He set the manuscript aside. "Before we get into my thoughts, what did he do that has you sitting in my living room in a sour mood? Don't you want to go say goodbye to Nelson before you head home to the city this afternoon?"

"He's working lunch to close at the restaurant today and I don't think he wants people gossiping about us. And with our parents coming up next weekend, that's just something he doesn't need."

"You talked to him about that?"

"Not exactly." Brandi fingered her thick wavy hair. She stared at the fireplace, which had a couple of logs and two candles for decorations. "We might have talked about being exclusive, but we didn't say anything about going out in public. He's so private, even with me. Besides, he's made it clear as the sky is blue, this won't last."

"How do you feel about that?"

"Honestly, right now I'm okay with it. I like that I can come here, kick back, read some manuscripts, and let loose a little. It's a stress-free relationship. I don't have all the craziness of having to totally answer to someone else, but all the benefits of being exclusive."

"Are you sure about that? Because I believe the only reason you went back to Ethan was to try to prove to yourself that Nelson meant nothing to you and now you're trying to act as if Nelson is still a passing fling." Lake lifted his arm and rested it on the back of the couch. They hadn't talked about it since she'd mentioned it the other day, except that things had gone well and she planned on coming up more often. She wanted to spend time with her niece, but she also wanted to be with Nelson. To see where things could go. But every time she allowed her mind to go down that road, she was reminded of who she was and how her personal life often played out in public.

Ethan had political aspirations. He thrived in the environment, which always bothered her because she hated being in the spotlight. The only one in the family who actually enjoyed that was her mother.

"You were miserable all winter. Any time I tried to talk to you about it, you shut me down. You told me that I was meddling. I've never done that." Lake didn't often express his opinions about her personal life, even when asked.

She appreciated that about her brother. If she wanted him to insert himself, she'd tell him, and he'd let her know exactly what he thought. However, he never made her feel that if she made a different decision, it would be the wrong one.

Until now.

Except he didn't believe she should be with either man. Not really.

"I will admit I was conflicted, but I needed to be

sure I was done with Ethan because every time he came back to town, we hooked up. That's not healthy."

"You're right, it's not. But neither is being in a relationship with a man who's emotionally unavailable, which isn't much different than what you were doing with Ethan." Lake had a valid point, one she'd been thinking long and hard on.

Only, it brought her to one conclusion.

"I don't know that I am either," she said.

"What do you mean? You went through all the trouble to have a conversation with him about moving things to a different level and you just told me that you're enjoying the perks of being in an exclusive relationship. Why are you backpedaling?"

"Mom's movie premieres in three weeks. We both know our lives are going to be in the spotlight more than usual. And that movie is going to be a hit. The experts are already talking Oscars." She tilted her head. "Between Nelson not being the kind of man who is going to stand on the red carpet with me, I don't want my love life in the public eye. We can date in secret, enjoy each other until it's run its course, and then move on. No one will be the wiser."

"You're living in fantasyland if you think the last part of that statement is true." Lake raised his hands and laughed. "Trust me. I know all about not wanting to have your love life plastered all over the tabloids. I avoided having one because of it. But you can't avoid it. We're the children of Chandler and Phoebe Grant. We're always going to be in the public eye. Look at what happened to me and Tiki two months ago when someone decided to snap a picture of us buying stuff for our baby. It became headline news what we spent. It's ridiculous, but it's our life and truthfully, if you want privacy, you should have waited until after the Oscars at the end of the year to start anything up with Nelson. You're going to get caught. Some photographer is going to see you coming and going." Lake reached out and covered her mouth with his palm. "Now that I've heard your excuse, I call bullshit. You're afraid because you're falling for this guy so now you're talking yourself out of it."

"Now you're talking out of your ass." She swallowed her pulse. "I like him. A lot. But Dad is putting more pressure on me. I'm finally head of acquisitions. I make all the decisions on what we publish, with very few exceptions. I need to focus on our family company."

Lake squeezed her shoulder. "Do you hear yourself? You've flipped and flopped in one weekend."

"I have not. I never said I wanted to jump into discussions about marriage and kids. I'm not ready for that. With anyone, but especially not someone like Nelson." She leaned over and snagged the manuscript. "Can we talk about something else now?"

"Sure." Lake nodded. "But I'm always here to

lend an ear if you want. Oh." He raised his finger. "Am I supposed to play dumb around Nelson?"

"Nah. You're my brother. Besides, I get the feeling his brothers know about us. Just don't be an asshole."

"Who? Me?" He tapped his chest. "Never."

She laughed. "Moving on. Give me your insights on Marcus' manuscript and what wasn't executed right."

"After you tell me what he did that upset you." Lake took the papers from her hands and lifted the top sheet.

"He emailed me asking if I had the chance to finish it and if I could meet with him in person to discuss it before he leaves for North Carolina. He mentioned how much he enjoyed our discussion and really wanted to hear my feedback face-to-face."

"That's easy to say no to."

"He somehow found Dad's email and copied him on it."

"Shit. That's manipulative." Lake pinched the bridge of his nose. "Have you talked with Dad yet?"

"No. Since you've read the entire manuscript and have an opinion, I'll wait to hear what you have to say, and then I'll call Dad on the drive home."

"That's probably a good idea, especially since he's been good at not checking work email over the weekend these days." Lake leaned forward and lifted a pen from the coffee table. He tapped it against the paper. "Are you still thinking of asking for a revise and rewrite?"

"Absolutely."

"Totally agree. This is absolutely the wrong story. It's got all the right moving parts, but the ending left me wanting to toss the book across the room and never read anything by this man again. I mean, the widow kills the war hero because he let her husband die. But she had the affair. The author tries to redeem her, but it's impossible. Not the way it's written. It's frustrating because I loved the premise."

"So do I," she said. "But I can't decide if this should be a true military thriller and we focus on the mission. Get rid of the married couple and drop in some romantic storyline, with a baby that somehow puts the hero at risk. Or we make it a wartime romance."

"I like the latter. Make the husband the antagonist. A true bad guy and the affair is more a product of necessity. Especially since the heroine and the war hero have a history."

"I do like that and it means less work for the author," Brandi said. "Might be a better move to make those suggestions right out of the gate."

"You're right. Even those could be an extensive rewrite. But it also stays closer to his original idea, which we both loved."

"I need to finish this novel and send him an extensive revision letter by next weekend," she said. "I just wish I knew what he thought he was accomplishing by copying Dad."

"Who knows." Lake handed her the manuscript with his notes. "I know you don't like looking at my ideas until after you're done, but take them. Call me if you want to talk." He tilted his head. "You know. We need someone who can walk us through the military portion of this and it can't be anyone Marcus knows."

"We have expert contacts. Other ex-military authors."

"But no one who went to West Point or was a Green Beret. Nelson and his brothers all went to West Point and were Delta Force. They could be excellent consultants."

In the background, a baby wailed.

Lake jumped to his feet. "I can tell by that scrunched-up look on your face you're not sure about the idea. Take a few days to think about it and we can discuss it later in the week."

The sound of the baby crying got louder and louder.

Lake glanced over his shoulder. "I better go. It was a rough night and if I can hold this child off even a half hour before feeding time, Tiki might be willing to have another one someday."

"If our princess mother can manage to have two, Tiki will be able to push through this with flying colors." Before the last word came out of her mouth, her brother was gone. Setting aside the papers, she opened her laptop and found her spot in the manuscript. She'd respond to Marcus tomorrow, during business hours.

Her cell buzzed four minutes after she started reading. She glanced at the screen with the intention of ignoring it.

Shit.

Her mother.

As much as she'd prefer to wait until she was in the car, she knew her mother would then move to Lake and that was the last thing he needed.

She tapped the green button. "Hi, Mom. Can I call you back in a couple of hours when I get in the car?"

"This will only take a second of your time."

"Okay." Nothing ever took only a few minutes when it came to Phoebe Grant. "What's up?"

"I'm worried about the disruption my visit will cause in Lake and Tiki's life next weekend. We were able to fly under the radar a bit last time, but there's no way we can now. I'm making appearances left and right. Your father and I can't go anywhere without camera lights flashing. It's only going to get worse once the movie premieres."

"Lake and his wife's family have an excellent relationship with the state police. The house has a state-of-the-art security system. You and Dad have both asked the press to leave your children alone, while making yourselves accessible. It's going to be fine."

"I think we should get ahead of it all."

"Ahead, how?" Brandi shut her laptop, set it aside, and stood. She made her way across the room and pulled open the sliders. Stepping out onto the deck, she sucked in a deep breath. The temperature had dropped to fifty degrees. Bending over, she clicked on the gas firepit and curled up on the chaise lounge and sighed.

"I want to have a premiere party."

"Excuse me?" Brandi sat straight up. She coughed. "Isn't that scheduled already?"

"The studio set one up, but I've been given permission to have a private viewing for family and close friends. In Lake George so my son and his wife can attend."

That did make sense considering Lake and Tiki weren't sure they would both be able to make it.

"You want to do this next weekend?"

"Yes. The studio will reach out to the village theater. I'll need a little help with the guest list because I'll want to invite all of Tiki's family. I was also thinking of seeing if we could rent out Blue Moon. Do you think that's possible? You've met the owners, right?"

Brandi set the cell on the railing and tapped speaker. She rubbed her temples. "I don't know if they'd close it down for a private party. That might be asking a lot."

"We'd make it worth their while," her mother said

with that pleading voice that got under Brandi's skin. "Could you or your brother ask them for us before you head back to the city? It should be on Saturday, but we could do Friday or Sunday. Whatever works best for them. However, I need to know today."

Brandi let out a long sigh. "I'll see what I can do." She knew there was no arguing with her mother.

"If you can book it, your dad said you can work from up there until this is over. That way none of the details will fall on Lake."

"Mom. Your publicity isn't my job."

"It is when Dad agreed to publish my autobiography."

"He did what?" She glared at the cell. "I mean, I know I told you that I'd be on board, but we haven't even discussed it yet."

"Relax, honey. It's years away from happening. Just be glad that I'm helping pave the way for you to spend more time working from home than having to be at the office every day. Publishing is changing and there's no reason why you can't have different office hours if you want."

"I appreciate you championing me, Mom. But next time, please let me fight my own battles with Dad."

Her mom let out a sweet little chuckle. "You know it didn't work that way with Lake and it's not going to work that way with you. Now, I best be going. Let me know what you find out about Blue Moon. Love you."

The line went dead.

She lifted her phone and pulled up Nelson's contact information.

Brandi: *Are you busy? If I stopped by, would you have a half hour or so to talk some business with me?*

Nelson: *Business? I'm intrigued.*

Brandi: *You might not be when I tell you what my family wants. Be there in forty-five?*

Nelson: *Looking forward to your proposition.*

Brandi: *Get your mind out of the gutter. It's not like that. Unless you suddenly got a lock on that office door.*

Nelson: *I'll see what I can do between now and the time you get here.*

She snagged her phone and stuffed it in her back pocket. This could potentially change things between them, at least in the short term.

6

Nelson sat on his lower patio near the dock, under the gazebo, sipping his coffee, trying not to jump in his boat and make a massive wave as he drove way too close to Marcus and his crew.

Motherfuckers.

"Hey," Maverick's voice echoed from behind.

He turned and nodded. Both his brothers strolled down the steps. They'd all purchased homes within a one-mile radius on Assembly Point, though it had taken a year for that to happen, along with overpaying. But they didn't care. They were lucky to have been born into privilege and even luckier to have never taken advantage of it until now, making it easier for their parents to part with a few dollars to ensure their sons put down roots.

Even if it wasn't with a woman.

"There's a whole pot of coffee inside if you want some." Nelson held up his mug.

"I'll go grab two," Maverick said.

"Thanks." Phoenix leaned against the post and folded his arms. "That's one of The Heritage Inn boats."

"Reese texted me last night, informing me that Marcus had one booked from six to noon and that the private eye—with the help of his cleaning staff—would be doing a little digging in at least Marcus' room."

"Has she started?"

"Yup." Nelson had been having a conversation with Reese ever since he noticed Marcus outside his house. "Reese gave those assholes five popular fishing spots."

"Off your dock isn't one of them," Phoenix said. "When is Brandi coming back?"

"Sometime this evening." If Nelson included today, he had three days before the Saturday movie premiere for *A Girl Named Lilly*. Agreeing to be the host to the private event should have been a no-brainer. The free publicity alone was worth the price of admission had it not been for Marcus.

And his goddamned fucking book.

Nelson had to find out what was in it and why Marcus was really in town. Something told him the two of them were tied together.

"I told her she could stay with me. She hasn't

decided if she's going to take me up on that offer. She's worried about the media."

Maverick appeared with a carafe of coffee. He refilled Nelson's and then poured himself and Phoenix each a mug before making himself comfortable by sitting on the railing. "The media should be our friend in this."

"Except for them." Nelson glanced at his cell. "If the PI doesn't find this manuscript, I might have to break down and come clean with Brandi."

"You're going to have to do that with her eventually, anyway." Phoenix lowered his chin and sipped.

Maverick smirked.

"It's still a fling." Nelson gulped. "We're just not seeing other people."

"You can tell yourself that if it helps you sleep at night, but you're falling for her, hard," Maverick said. "And there's no fault in that."

Phoenix laughed. "This coming from the guy who says he's never wanted a woman."

"No." Maverick raised his finger. "I said that I've got all that I've ever wanted and I don't want to rock the boat by adding unnecessary conflict. Women bring on the crazy."

Nelson stared at the foursome as they sat quietly in their boat, holding their fishing poles, wearing baseball caps, not gazing in his direction.

Or so it seemed.

"I'm tempted to confront Marcus and ask him

point-blank what the fuck his game is, but I'm not sure what the point would be. He's just going to lie." Nelson dumped out the rest of his coffee. "I don't want to put Brandi in an impossible situation. Having a vendetta against me has nothing to do with her."

"Marcus would comprise her company." Phoenix cocked his head. "And yes, we'd go after him if he lied about you at all."

"What would be really nice was if Marcus would go back to the rock he crawled out from under." Nelson set his mug aside and gripped the railing. "You both agree I'm not being paranoid, even though we've found nothing."

"We agree," Phoenix said.

"I'm sure they have seen the three of us standing here." Nelson turned. "If I say anything, it's going to create a problem for Brandi. I can't have that. However, either of you can do it on my behalf, as if I don't know."

"I can make that work," Maverick said. "Marcus and I've had words before."

"I remember." Nelson shook his head. "You shouldn't have gone after him."

Maverick raised his hands. "He's lucky I didn't beat his ass, but the point is, he'd believe I'd go behind your back."

"I'll cover this morning," Phoenix said. "Maverick can go to the hotel around noon and have a little chat with our friends."

"I'll work until Brandi gets into town, unless she's not staying with me. Then we can adjust." Nelson took one more glance over his shoulder. "I wish I believed nothing was going to come of this so I could put my past to bed, but I know that's not the case."

Brandi stuffed her laptop into her bag and lifted it to her shoulder. She sucked in a deep breath and headed down the long corridor toward her father's office, pausing to glance in what was still Lake's workspace. Until four weeks before Maddie was born, Lake came into the city once a month for at least three or four days for editorial and creative meetings.

More and more editors were allowed to work from home at least twice weekly. This was at her directive. Her father reluctantly gave her the green light on the condition that if the quality and the quantity of work diminished, everyone would return to the office.

She could envision a hybrid office and wanted to expand its reach. They had already pulled five indie authors from self-publishing and offered them the best of both worlds. Why not hire independent content editors? Her father had always been concerned about going with a digital-only line. He believed because of how successful indie authors had become, that wasn't a road any author would want to take.

But discoverability was still an issue for everyone.

That, and costs.

However, she believed there was a way to do it that could benefit everyone. It wasn't about pushing out a million titles, hoping one sticks. No. It was about finding a select few—the elite.

It meant getting some named authors to come over to the dark side.

She squared her shoulders and tapped on her father's door. It always seemed so massive. "You wanted to see me before I left."

"Come in and close the door."

Whenever her dad asked her to do that, her heart raced like she was a teenager again and she'd been caught sneaking in after curfew. She set her bag on the floor between the two chairs in front of her father's desk before easing into the one on the right. She preferred that one because it forced her father to push his monitor to the side.

Which he did immediately.

Of course, he left his computer open, meaning he could become distracted anytime.

Typical.

She smoothed down the front of her slacks.

"Is something wrong?"

"I'm concerned about a couple of things." Her father clasped his hands together and rested them on the wood surface. "I'm going to start with this author who copied me on an email over the weekend."

"I've been meaning to talk to you about that, but Mom has me running in circles."

"I know. I know. And I'm sorry this week is so stressful for you. Once this premiere is over, everything will be thrust back to Mom's publicity team." Her dad nodded, holding his hand up. "I appreciate all that you're doing. I wouldn't have stuck my nose in this if the party hadn't fallen in your lap."

"It's sweet that Mom wanted to make sure Lake and Tiki could attend, and to include all of Tiki's family, but this is a lot."

"It wasn't your mother's idea." He flattened his hands on the desk and stood. Turning, he faced the window and folded his arms. "I don't know why this bothers me, but her publicist came up with the idea. She mentioned her team thought it would be great for Mom's image. They are really pushing this Oscar thing."

"I don't disagree with Leslie. I might not like it, but it will be good for Mom and the movie."

"Lake isn't thrilled. He doesn't want to put his family on display and I don't blame him. He's going along in part because his wife is a good person and wants to support her mother-in-law."

"Dad, it's more than that. We all know this is Mom's very last movie, television show, Broadway spot, anything. She has no desire to do it anymore. She's turned down three scripts already. All she wants to do is be Granny."

Her father turned. "I'm so excited for your mom. This means the world to her and I'm happy to be by her side. I wish she'd listened to her instincts, said no to this premiere, and kept it in the city."

"It will be good for a lot of businesses in the village of Lake George. We must do our best to ensure those who want to remain out of the public eye, do."

Her dad waggled his finger. "That brings me back to why I wanted to talk to you." Leaning over his desk, he turned his computer and tapped at the keyboard. "Please understand I wasn't going behind your back. This isn't because I don't trust you to do what's best for this company, because I do. It's only because of the position that your mother and I put you in."

"Get to the point, Dad."

"I wanted to know why this man felt the need to tag me in a correspondence when he hadn't been signed. You know how I feel about shit like that."

Oh boy, did she. Her dad hated it when people played games. If you had a problem with the way someone handled something, you took it up with them. If you couldn't settle it, then you went to their superior, but you did it in a professional manner.

"I thought his email to you was strange and I couldn't figure out why he'd copy me. If he had romantic intentions, that's not the way to get your attention. If he thought it would push your hand, well, that just shows how little he understands the business. So I went back and read the correspondence."

"You could have just asked me." She tilted her head.

"I stopped in your office three times on Monday and twice this morning. You've been busy." He arched a brow. "Anyway, he doesn't have an agent and you met him at the conference where you ended up not listening to any pitches."

"His was the only manuscript worth taking a full look at."

"I didn't read it more than the first scene and the synopsis." Her dad sat back down, rolling his chair closer. "It's good. But there's a problem."

"What's that?"

He tapped on the keyboard. "His sister's husband was a Navy SEAL. His name was Seth Baxter. The details of what happened are still classified."

"He was up front with me about that detail, but assured me that was the only factual part in the novel, but I plan on informing him—through email—that we will need verification from the military that we can publish his book. But only if he can handle the rewrite I'm going to be asking for."

"Good, because the ending he has planned is depressing as shit."

"Agreed."

"I was thinking we could ask the owners of Blue

Moon to consult on the mission aspects of this novel," she said. "They went to West Point. All ended up Delta Force. They could be a good source of information for our thriller line."

"Perhaps, but I don't know about this book." He tapped his finger on screen. "I'm not sure we can trust them."

Standing, she leaned closer. "What am I looking at?"

"A picture I found on Roxy Baxter's social media."

"Who is that?"

"The widow and Marcus' sister," her father said. "At one point, she was involved with Nelson."

Blinking, she lifted the computer. Using the trackpad, she made the image bigger. It was a picture of a group of people. Nelson's hair had been buzzed, and he was in his fatigues. He looked young. He had one arm around the girl in question and his free hand held a beer.

One of his brothers was in the background.

Marcus was there.

As were the men he'd introduced her to at Blue Moon, along with other men and women.

Setting the computer down, she eased into the chair.

"Did you know that Marcus and Nelson knew each other?"

"No." She swallowed. "There really isn't any reason for Nelson to tell me. I've never seen him and

Marcus together, although my meeting with Marcus was at Blue Moon."

"Don't you find that strange?"

"It's peculiar," she admitted. "But the only reason I told you and Mom about Nelson was because of this party. We're not out in the open. It's barely even a thing."

"I get you're being discreet. What I don't understand is why Nelson wouldn't tell you that he knows someone you could be working with."

She sighed. "He did ask me questions about what I was working on and I shut him down, so he could be simply following my lead. Respecting my business."

"Perhaps," her father said. "There are maybe a dozen pictures that show this Roxy girl with Nelson from about ten years ago. After that, there is no trace of Nelson anywhere in her social media. No reference to him. No connection whatsoever. And he doesn't have a presence at all. Nor do his brothers. Marcus, on the other hand, has a small one thanks to his wife."

Brandi took in a long, slow breath through her nose. She exhaled through her mouth. "What exactly are you getting at?"

"I only read the synopsis. But I have been reading your notes." He arched a brow. "Any chance there is more truth in this novel? Could Nelson be a character?"

"You think he's the man the heroine had an affair with?"

Her father shrugged. "I don't know." He waved his hand over the computer. "But something doesn't add up and I'm worried about what you might be walking into."

She stood. "Don't because I'm going to get to the bottom of it."

"I didn't tell you this because I wanted you to go off half-cocked." Her dad planted his hands on his hips. "I want you to send the revise and submit letter and see how Marcus responds. If he's willing to make our changes, we're being paranoid, and then you can deal with Nelson and why he chose not to mention his history with Marcus in your own way and we can send to legal regarding the mission before we make an offer."

"No, Dad. I'm not going to play that game. I'm going to ask Nelson that question now. And I'll send the letter. As a matter of fact, I'll do it now. I've got it written."

"I saw that."

She bent over, pulling her computer out. She'd wanted to run it by Lake, but only out of respect, since she'd used some of his notes. However, he'd understand. Quickly, she reread the letter, making sure it said exactly what she wanted, adding in the line that she would be available by email only if he had any questions. When she was done, she hit send. "There we go."

"Just be careful. I don't like games."

"I don't either and if Marcus has a problem with our editorial notes or disrespects the industry by trying to pull me aside, I'll gladly cut him loose."

"What about Nelson?"

"That's an entirely different situation and until I know more, there's nothing to even be upset over." Only, she felt betrayed. It wasn't a downright lie, but he omitted a fact and that left a bitter taste in her mouth.

7

Nelson had been on some dangerous missions. He'd been shot at. Stabbed. Electrocuted. Hell, he'd even died once.

His military training taught him to be calm and focused.

However, for the last few hours, he'd been useless. He started out in the office doing paperwork and couldn't keep his mind on the task at hand. He then moved on to manual labor. For a while, that worked until he started putting things away where they didn't belong. It wasn't a big deal, but he'd never been so jittery in all his life.

He resented the sensation.

So, he'd given up doing anything that required his attention. Instead, he sat in the far corner of the outside patio and stared at the lake while picking at some fries. He glanced at his watch. It was four in the afternoon. He'd hung out at his place until nearly two. That's how long those assholes floated in front of his dock. He'd wanted to jump in his boat a dozen times and be a dick by creating waves, but he'd promised his brothers he'd do nothing that could be considered a provocation.

So, he sat at home with his laptop, researching Marcus.

He found very little on his own and decided to pull in an old buddy whom he'd served with in Delta Force. A man named Dylan Sarich.

Dylan had retired about five years ago and now worked for an organization called The Aegis Network. If anyone could find the cracks in a man's past, it was Dylan and his three brothers, who also worked for the same company.

The intel had started to trickle in, but nothing stood out.

"You need to relax. You're wound tighter than Veronica." Phoenix smiled at the hostess as she weaved through the tables, her hips swaying back and forth with her skirt kicking up, showing off her toned legs. She sat a couple next to one of the heaters, placing the menus on the table.

She was a real looker with her long red hair, big green eyes, and curvy figure. But it was her killer personality that men—and women—responded to. No matter what was happening in her life, she was always in a good mood and had a natural gift of spreading that good cheer to others.

"That's a really bad comparison." Nelson took the beer that his brother offered. They rarely drank while at the restaurant, but today he'd bend the rules because his brother had a valid point.

He needed to relax.

"She's not uptight. She's just a fucking happy person all the time." Nelson tipped his beer. He took a sip and checked his cell, which he'd left faceup on the table.

Nothing from Maverick.

Fuck.

"I wish we could have set Maverick up with a listening device," Nelson mumbled.

"I'm not going to comment on that." Phoenix shifted, moving a second chair, and stretched out his leg.

"Good choice." Nelson chuckled. While he remained on high alert, his nerves settled having his brother close. "I don't like that a couple of the Grant's guests will be staying at The Heritage Inn."

"They're not guests. They work for the publicist. We've got a private eye living there and Reese and his wife are our eyes and ears," Phoenix said. "I doubt anyone in Brandi's family will step foot on The Heritage Inn property. They are all staying with Lake and his wife. Or Foster's rental."

"What if Marcus manages an invite to the

premiere? Then what?" Nelson's cell buzzed. Quickly, he lifted it, tapping the screen. "Marcus was able to avoid Maverick and now the foursome is headed south. Maverick is a half a mile behind them." Nelson lifted his beverage and chugged half of it. "Marcus is enjoying fucking with us. I just wish I knew his endgame," Nelson said. "Dylan was able to dig up a few things about Roxy's boyfriend and the fact they took a trip up here the week we started renovations."

"That's convenient."

Nelson tilted his head and rubbed his eyes. "Shit. Brandi's here and she doesn't look happy."

Brandi stood on the other side of the patio with Veronica who pointed in his direction. Brandi adjusted her bag and scowled as she marched across the wood planks.

"That's my cue to leave." Phoenix slipped into the main bar area through the service door.

Nelson stood, but his heart dropped to his feet. He swallowed. "I didn't expect to see you for another few hours at my place." His cell buzzed. He glanced down.

Maverick: *Marcus just pulled into the parking lot.*

Fuck.

"We need to talk," Brandi said.

"Why don't we go somewhere more private." He placed his hand on the small of her back.

She tensed.

That wasn't a good sign.

He dropped his arm to his side. "We can go up to the…" He paused midstep as he locked gazes with Marcus. Nelson had never been so happy to have not been touching his girlfriend. His spine stiffened.

Marcus tilted his head and smiled. "Oh my. My editor and my old friend. I didn't know the two of you knew each other."

"Anyone who has spent any amount of time in the area knows the Snow brothers and Blue Moon," Brandi said. "My family has booked their establishment for a private party this weekend and I'm here to discuss the details." Her tight tone wasn't lost on Nelson.

"I left you a voice message about twenty minutes ago," Marcus said. "I need to discuss your revision letter with you."

"I'm sorry, Marcus. Like I told you, any questions or concerns you have, please email me."

"I promise not to take up too much of your time. Perhaps breakfast tomorrow. Or lunch. You have to eat sometime," Marcus said.

Nelson wanted to intervene, but it wasn't his place. Besides, he was enjoying the way Brandi handled herself with confidence, even though a heavy dose of anger slipped out.

"This week is crazy for me. Also, I made an exception the first time because I had been unable to take pitches. I felt I owed you that. However, you are not one of our authors. The point of a revise and resubmit is to see how you handle our suggestions. If you want to discuss them, we can do so in email. And for the record, we won't be publishing the novel as written. I'm sorry to be blunt, but I'm running on limited time and I need to meet with Nelson regarding my mother's party."

"I hope you'll change your mind and meet with me." Marcus turned his attention to Nelson. "You and your brothers work way too much. Me and the boys want to get a poker game going and we'd like you to join."

"We have a rule; one of us always has to be at Blue Moon."

"Come on, man. This place runs itself."

"Sorry. Not with this party coming up."

"I've got an idea," Marcus said. "Why don't we play here? That way if something needs your attention, one of you can deal with it."

"I'll think about it."

"Wonderful." Marcus turned and followed Veronica to a table, his three buddies one pace behind.

Brandi stormed up the stairs and threw open the office door. She tossed her bag on the chair. Making her way to the window that overlooked the main bar, she folded her arms. "I don't know why I'm so pissed, but I am."

"At me or him?"

She laughed. "Both, but for different reasons."

He sat on the corner of his desk and folded his arms. "Marcus and I are not friends. We never really were."

"You had to have seen me with him the day I met with Delaney."

He nodded.

"Why didn't you tell me you knew a potential author of mine?"

"I didn't think it was going to be necessary unless you signed him and even then, your publishing company has nothing to do with me." He raked a hand across the top of his head. He had no idea how much of the truth he should reveal. There were things that legally he couldn't tell. He'd have to dance around those topics carefully. "In all honesty, I figured he'd be gone before it mattered and I'd never see him again."

"He leaves Sunday, right?"

"That's what he says." Nelson rolled his neck. "The last time he and I saw each other we ended up in a fistfight."

She turned and scowled.

Again.

"Are you kidding me?"

"Not my proudest moment, but if it makes you feel better, I didn't throw the first punch."

"I can't say that it does," she said.

"I was shocked that of all the places he and his buddies could have come for a bachelor weekend, they chose Lake George. Call me paranoid, but I don't believe in coincidences."

"You believe he came here for you?" Her brows shot up. "That's a little egotistical."

"Our history is a complicated one and some of it I legally can't get into. Much of what I did for the military is still classified."

"That, I understand. But you grilled me about a submission I was reading and thinking back on it, you suspected it was Marcus' manuscript."

"Grilled is a big word and I didn't pressure you into telling me anything about it, but yes, I knew Marcus had sent you a novel."

"How?"

"He told me," Nelson admitted.

"Why do you care?"

"Because I dated his sister." His stomach soured. At one point, he truly cared for Roxy. She'd been the one girl in his past that he thought he could have fallen in love with, but Marcus always got in the way. He had his sister's ear and he did everything he could to destroy his relationship with Roxy.

All because Nelson got a medal on a mission and Marcus didn't. That set off a chain of events—in Marcus' eyes—that lead to promotion after promotion for Nelson.

Marcus had become so resentful that Nelson

outranked him and had been given his own command and that's when the shit really hit the fan.

Next thing Nelson knew, Roxy had become jealous for no reason at all, always believing that he was cheating or lying to her about what he was doing and where he was going. If he left town to go visit his brothers, she believed both Maverick and Phoenix were covering for him while he visited one of his many girlfriends.

All bullshit.

He could never prove that her brother put those ideas in her head, and she never admitted it.

"I was prepared for you to lie about knowing her." Brandi blew out a puff of air as she held up her cell.

"Wow. That's an old picture," he said.

She fell back into the chair across from the desk. "What happened between you and Marcus' sister?"

"We dated for about two years. At the time I was a Green Beret and going to Ranger School with Marcus. He and I graduated from West Point together. We didn't get along then either. We're both competitive by nature, but he takes it to a new level."

"I'm not surprised by that statement."

"Long story short, he didn't like that Roxy and I were getting serious. He meddled. He won. I moved on and so did Roxy."

"Why do I get the feeling there's a lot more to that story than you're telling me." She pursed her lips.

He pinched the bridge of his nose. "You can't tell

me what's in that book; I can't—and I won't—tell you certain things about that time in my life."

"At least you're being honest."

"Can I ask you something about Marcus?"

She narrowed her stare. "I might not answer."

"Why won't you take a face-to-face meeting with him?"

"I can actually tell you that." She sat up taller, tucking her hair behind her ears. "I sent him what we call a revise and resubmit letter. What that means is I rejected the manuscript, but I liked the writing and the premise enough to give him an editorial letter. Depending on how he executes it…" She paused, tapping her fingers on her legs as if she were typing. "You want me to take the meeting."

"I think he's fucking with me and I would bet that he'd suggest meeting here so I could potentially overhear the discussion."

"You'd like that, wouldn't you?"

He rubbed the back of his neck, looking for the right words. "I'm not enjoying this, if that's what you're suggesting. But it would give us both something we need. You would know if what he's writing he can, and I'd know if he's writing about me."

"If anyone can see themselves in his characters, it could be considered libel, especially if it's not completely factual."

"If he's writing about what I think he is, there's some truth to it."

Her jaw dropped and her eyes went wide.

That told him all he needed to know.

Motherfucker.

Nelson gripped the side of his desk. His blood raced through his system like an out-of-control high-speed train. It wasn't that he cared if Brandi knew about what happened between him and Roxy, it was how in which the story had been told.

And the lies that were probably attached.

Brandi cleared her throat and stood. "If it's only some, even though it's fictionalized, if you can see yourself in it, and can prove it's you, it's still libel. Although, it's very hard to prove."

He opened his mouth, but she held up her hand.

"I won't publish anything that is questionable, no matter how good. My company has had enough controversy to last a lifetime. I don't want to take a meeting with Marcus. I feel like that's putting him in the driver's seat of whatever game he's playing. Besides, I've made it very clear to him that if he's not willing to make changes, then there is no deal."

"That's fair," he said. "I am concerned that he somehow knows about us and will come after you, to hurt me."

She leaned forward, resting her elbows on her knees. "You really believe he hates you that much."

"I know he does."

"I might have another way for you to see what's in the book and help me fact-check some military things, but I need to talk with my dad and brother first."

"All right." He nodded.

She stood, collecting her bag.

"Brandi, I'm sorry that you're stuck in the middle of this. I never meant to do that to you." He took her by the biceps.

"You didn't. Marcus did. But the moment you saw me with him and you believed he was out to hurt you, as your girlfriend, you should have told me."

"Point taken." He brushed his lips over hers in a tender kiss.

But it didn't last as she pulled away before it even got started.

"Will I see you later?" he asked.

"I'll text you after I've had a chance to visit with Lake, Tiki, and Maddie." She patted his chest. "For the record, I think what Marcus has done is a low blow, regardless of how he feels about you."

"Done?"

"To your character in his book. It's kind of obvious to me now and…" She shook her head and sighed. "I'll text you in a couple of hours." She turned and took five steps, pausing at the door. She glanced over her shoulder. "I've only known you a year and the truth is, I don't know you very well, but I've never seen you be violent."

"I'm generally not."

"You fought Marcus."

"He brings out the worst in me," Nelson added.

"Unless he hits you first—and there are witnesses to it—you better behave yourself."

"Yes, ma'am."

"Don't ever *ma'am* me if you want to see me naked again."

At least he knew there was still the possibility.

8

Brandi paced in front of her brother's desk in his home office. She tapped a pencil against her temple. "Daddy, we must find out if Marcus committed a crime regarding a classified mission."

"Sweetheart, you said yourself that Nelson didn't say much anyway," her father's voice boomed over the speakerphone.

"He didn't have to. He knows he's in that book, and I know what character he is, and so do both of you." She pointed to the cell and then to her brother. "If Marcus is out to hurt Nelson, he'll take this to another publisher if we turn him down. He might get someone to bite."

"The major players will do exactly what we would do and demand a letter from the military that states no part of this book is true," Lake said. "But Dad, I understand where Brandi is coming from. This is personal for Nelson. Let's say there is no truth to the special ops portion, whether it be another publisher or us, that's been verified. If there is any truth to what happened between the heroine and this Anderson character, and Nelson can see and prove that it's him, that opens us, or whoever takes on the project, to a libel suit."

"But bringing him on as a consultant could open a different can of worms," her father said.

"I disagree, Dad." She stopped pacing and stared at the phone as if her father were going to jump through the airwaves. "He tells us if Marcus screwed up regarding classified information. He also can confirm if he's been trashed in the book. If that's the case, we can find all sorts of reasons for rejecting the book that has nothing to do with Nelson while he does whatever he needs to do to protect his side of the story."

"But we fed him the ammunition he needs. And we did it knowing that Marcus could be running Nelson's name through the mud," her dad said. "I prefer the idea of you meeting with Marcus. Find out if he's even willing to revise. If he's not, cut him loose."

She shivered. "Doesn't Nelson have the right to know what's in that book?"

"If we do that, we're breaking a trust we might not ever be able to recover from," her dad said. "I know that's harsh, but we have to think about our writers and the future of this company."

"Dad's right on that point, but bringing Nelson and his brothers on as expert consultants will protect us." Lake leaned back in his big leather chair.

"That would be fine if your sister wasn't sleeping with him."

She stumbled backward, hitting her ass on Tiki's desk. Closing her eyes, she took in a deep, cleansing breath. Hearing her father discuss her love life was always unsettling, but this sounded unusually distasteful.

"I've got an idea," Lake said. "Reese is an ex-Marine. We could hire him as our new consultant. I know Nelson and him are friendly. Maybe Nelson would be willing to disclose his personal life enough that Reese could tell if it's libel or not."

"That might work," her father said. "Brandi, do you think you could talk Nelson and this Reese fellow into it?"

"I can try." She held her brother's gaze.

"I've got to run," her dad said. "Your mom needs me. Keep me informed of everything. And I mean every little damned detail."

"We will." Lake tapped the screen. "If Reese agrees, you know he will let Nelson read that manuscript."

"I'm counting on it."

The one thing Brandi hadn't anticipated was that Nelson would pull his brothers into the conversation.

Though she should have.

They were his support system and they knew him better than anyone.

She sat in an Adirondack chair before a warm fire and stared at the flames as they snaked toward the dark sky. Pulling the fleece blanket up to her chest, she did her best to be patient while Nelson, his brothers, and Reese passed back and forth the contract her father sent over.

"Do you have any questions?" She couldn't stand the silence a second longer.

"I don't have a problem with the contract." Reese lifted his wineglass and swirled. "It's straightforward."

She'd only met Reese a handful of times. She knew he was a quiet, contemplative man with a dry sense of humor who put his family and friends before anything.

"What concerns me is that we could be playing right into his hand," Reese said.

"I was thinking the same thing." Nelson stood next to the big tree by the gazebo. He held his wineglass and sipped. "Marcus is incredibly intelligent. When we were at West Point, I got better grades than he did because he was a smart-ass. He often got pleasure from debating with the professors. That was never a good look."

"Unless it was debate class," Phoenix added.

Nelson chuckled. "Even then, he had a reputation for being a dick. He got off on pushing people's buttons. He'd argue for the sake of arguing. He loved to take the opposing viewpoint. When I first met him, I thought that was ingenious. I've always believed that to understand your value system, you need to be able to defend the other side. But he did it to tear people down. To strip them of their core beliefs. He could be cruel."

"I knew men like him in the Marines. They believed if they broke you, they could rebuild you into a better version of yourself. Only, their idea of what a man or woman should be was never good." Reese took the pen and signed on the dotted line, handing her the contract. "Regardless of whether we handle the situation this way or a different way, I'm happy to be a consultant for your company anytime. I can help with military and state police. But you might want to get Jared on board with that. He keeps rumbling he wants to retire in a couple of years. That would be a good side gig for him."

"Thanks. I'll extend the offer," she said.

"That goes for all of us," Nelson said. "If your family will have us."

"That's my decision, and I'll print out more copies. Our editors will be thrilled. It's hard to find experts willing to do the legwork, but you make it sound like there's another option when dealing with this awkward situation with Marcus."

"We could let this play out." Reese polished off his beverage, setting the glass on the tray.

"That's putting Marcus in the driver's seat," Phoenix said. "I don't like giving him that much control. He's been a thorn in my brother's side for years. He's threatened to take him down. To ruin him."

"I didn't know that." Brandi shifted her gaze.

Nelson looked out toward the water. "Until now, I thought they were empty threats."

"Not true," Maverick said. "It's always been in the back of your mind."

"The further away I got from what happened—from seeing him—the more I believed we could all move past it." Nelson downed the rest of his wine.

"I don't know what is true and what is fiction. And that's frustrating as hell," she mumbled.

"Here's the thing," Reese said. "Once Brandi sends me that contract back, she can forward me the manuscript. I'll know what it says and that will give us leverage, but we don't have to do anything with that information. We can let Marcus believe he's going to fuck Nelson seven ways to Sunday."

"I don't understand something." Brandi read the novel. The implication that Nelson had an affair wasn't necessarily a big deal. People did that every day. Considering it was with his ex-girlfriend didn't make it forgivable, but it made it relatable. "And maybe you can't clarify, but outside of a breach in classified material, all this does—"

"It goes to my discharge," Nelson said. "Not that the Army is going to strip me of my honorable discharge now, but it's possible they could have given me a less than honorable discharge at the time I left."

"I don't believe so," Maverick said. "I can see how we all might think it could apply, but Dad's lawyers all told us that it wouldn't."

"Yeah, but I know the story they were going to spin." Nelson reached for the bottle and poured himself another glass. "If she could have made that stick, there was a chance I could have gone to prison."

"Jesus," Brandi muttered. Her mind spun a few different scenarios, but landed flatly on one.

The accusation of rape.

She swallowed. She was a firm believer that no one should shame the victim. That women didn't cry rape. No one would want to put themselves through that kind of scrutiny because half the time people didn't believe the victim.

However, she found herself in a difficult position and she needed answers to some tough questions. "I can't do this anymore."

"Do what?"

"Pretend that I didn't read that book and that I don't know what we're talking about."

"Can you all give me a few minutes with Brandi, alone?" Nelson asked.

Reese stood. "I need to get home to my wife and kids. Call me in the morning."

"We're going to head out too," Maverick said.

"Text us with how you want to handle the workload tomorrow. We can be flexible." Phoenix squeezed Nelson's shoulder.

"I'll check in with you later," Nelson said.

Brandi pulled the fleece tighter around her body. The fire crackled. Sparks danced in the night sky. A few boats hummed along the shoreline. The red wine warmed her belly and dulled her senses.

She wasn't sure if that was a good thing or a bad thing.

"Would it be better if we printed out another copy of that contract and signed it?" Nelson asked. "I don't want to put your company in a compromising situation."

"I don't want to know about the mission. I want to know about your relationship with Roxy and I want to know everything."

"That's the problem, they are intertwined."

"Did we agree to be exclusive?"

He nodded.

"Doesn't that make us a couple?" she asked.

"Yes," he said. "But there are still things I can't tell you. That wouldn't even change if you were my wife."

"I can't ask you questions based on what I read. I

need you to tell me." She pinched the bridge of her nose. "Please. I'm begging you to give me what you can."

"You want to know if I slept with Roxy while she was married to Seth?"

"Did you?"

"Yes," he whispered. "I'm not proud of what happened. I don't regret many things in life, but that is one decision I wish I could reverse."

"Why'd you do it?"

He tugged his chair closer and took her hands. "I have no good answer to that."

"Who initiated it?"

"She did." He held her gaze. "But that doesn't absolve me of my actions. She was married. It doesn't matter what she told me was going on in her life; I should have kept with my original answer."

"Did she get pregnant?"

"That's where things get tricky," he said. "She had a miscarriage after her husband died. Seth had been deployed for a month before I slept with her and the math added up to when we were together, but I can't be totally sure it was mine."

She squeezed Nelson's hands. "I need you to sign that contract. I want you to read that book so you can tell me everything. And I need a stronger drink."

"I'm not sure I want to," Nelson said.

She poked him dead center in the chest. "I don't care. You're going to do it for me and you're going to do it tonight." She jumped to her feet, dropping the fleece to the ground. "I'm going to go get shit-faced. I'm sleeping in your bed, alone. It's going to take you all night and maybe into tomorrow to finish."

"Where am I going to get a copy?"

"You've got paper and a printer, right?"

"Yeah," he said.

"Make sure it's full. I'll start printing."

9

Nelson tapped on the master bedroom door. "Brandi? You awake? I've got coffee." He'd respected her wishes and left her alone all night. He'd also managed to skim through Marcus' massive novel without leaving the house and strangling the bastard.

Although, he did kick a tree.

Throw a chair.

And do two shots before he realized this wasn't Marcus' endgame. It was all a distraction.

He heard a groan as he pushed open the door a little wider. "Are you okay?" He strolled across the room, staring at the sleeping beauty, who pulled the covers over her head. Setting down two mugs, he poured the bitter brew from the carafe. "What did you do all night while I read a bunch of crap?" Sitting on the side of the bed, he tugged at the comforter.

"I couldn't fall asleep, so I drank tequila. There's a reason I don't consume that shit."

He laughed. "I could put some Baileys in this." He pushed the mug under her nose. "It might help the hangover."

"No. Some caffeine, water, and something very greasy will do the trick." She pushed herself to a sitting position, wrapping the sheet and blanket around her waist, showing off a white tank top with no bra.

He forced his gaze back to her gorgeous green-blue eyes. If they could get through the half-truths in Marcus' book, then there would be plenty of time to explore whatever their relationship would be moving forward.

"What time is it?" She palmed the cup and brought it to her lips. Blowing slowly, she took a sip. "Mmmm, that's good."

"It's almost noon."

Her eyes grew wide. "You're joking."

"Nope. I kept waiting for you to show your pretty face."

"You should have woken me up sooner." She reached for her cell. "My dad is probably going nuts. So is my mom. I always check messages first thing in the morning."

"Lake called me at eight wondering what was going on."

She glared. "What did you tell him?"

"I asked him to stall your parents."

"You had no right to do that." She poked him in the chest.

"Ouch. That hurt." He scowled. "Maybe not. But I wanted to finish the book and I thought maybe if your parents thought you were busy with details for the premiere and other things, that would give us a chance to clear the air about things."

"You actually stayed up and finished it?"

"I can't say I read every single word, but yeah."

"Wow. I'm impressed." She took another sip before setting the cup on the nightstand. She snagged a pillow and hugged it.

"Don't be. I burned it."

She laughed. "I'm sorry." She covered her mouth. "I know that's not funny."

"I almost wish he'd discussed a mission that was still classified, but he didn't. He kept the details vague and switched up so many things that I would guess the Army would approve, except for the things about me."

"So, his character, Anderson, is actually truly you."

"Anderson is my middle name," he said.

"Jesus. That's too close for comfort." She tucked her hair behind her ears. "Is what he writes the truth?"

"It's mostly lies, wrapped in half-truths. But there's enough there about my past with Roxy and what happened after her husband died that anyone who knows us could guess that he's writing about me. Especially if he ties his name to it."

"He never said anything about writing under a pen name." She pressed her hand on his stomach, lifting his shirt. "You have a lot of scars. I asked you once about them and you made light of them."

"Defense mechanism."

"I gathered." She traced her finger over a few of them. "I know you said that Marcus did a good job with—"

"I will tell you the things that are true about me that were portrayed in that assassination." He curled his fingers around her wrist and brought her palm to his lips. "As I told you, Roxy and I dated ten years ago. I cared for her greatly. It was probably the only real relationship I had. If there was any woman in my past that I could say I had true feelings for, it would have to be her."

She narrowed her stare. "That's a hard pill to swallow."

"It is for me too." Carefully, he climbed over her with his coffee, fluffing a pillow and stretching out his legs. "Marcus did a lot of things to break us up. Eventually, it worked. I didn't see Roxy for years, but I had to deal with Marcus."

"Were you and Marcus on the same team?"

"No. But we did go through Special Forces

training together. We also did a couple of JSOC missions."

"What's that?"

"It stands for Joint Special Operations Command. It's when the CIA, the FBI, or any other organization utilizes a special team comprised of different branches for highly sensitive missions."

"In the book, Anderson goes to Brooke. He seduces her and it's a gross scene."

"I couldn't read it," he admitted. "Although, I did laugh when Brooke killed me in the end."

"We're getting sidetracked," she said.

"Okay. What's true is that I died and was brought back to life while on a mission." He pressed his finger over her lips. "I don't think that's technically classified, but I wouldn't repeat it."

"I'm not going to," she said. "But I gather you were part of the search and rescue team."

"I can't comment on that." He lowered his chin.

"Fair enough," she said. "But he implies you killed her husband."

"Again, this gets into a gray area." He set his mug down. "But it's not true. I think this entire fucking novel is a distraction. I don't know from what, but Marcus doesn't intend to use it to hurt me. I bet he knew you'd never want to publish it. All he needed was to get a foot in the door."

"Why me?"

"We learned that Roxy was up here with her new

boyfriend about the same time we started renovations on Blue Moon."

"That was long before you and I started seeing each other."

"True, but Marcus and Roxy had to have known my brothers and I have been living here which means they could know about us," he said.

"I'm struggling with why Marcus would spend the time to write a novel. Do you have any idea how long it takes? Or what authors go through? It's not easy."

"I don't have a clue," he admitted. "But the more I think about everything, the more I believe that something else is at play."

"I don't know. He could take his book to another publisher."

"But fiction can't hurt me." Nelson had been so blinded by rage when he tossed the pages into the fire he hadn't been thinking straight. "Even if his end goal were to get someone to print that mess, he's not pushing it as truth. He even states in his acknowledgment page that it's all false."

"That's true. He does have a disclaimer." She tilted her head. "Is he just messing with you?"

"No. I don't believe that for one second. He's got a plan and it involves destroying me, and most likely my brothers too. But now we have to figure out what that is, and I fear you're going to end up collateral damage."

"If he ruins my mother's party, I'll wring his neck."

"We need to speak with the publicist that made the recommendation for this premiere, because it couldn't come at a worse time," he said.

"Leslie will be here tomorrow. She's staying at The Heritage Inn."

"I don't like that." He shook his head. "How long has she worked for your mom?"

"Ten years," Brandi said. "She's rock solid and totally loyal to my family. She helped us deal with Lake and Tiki's scandal two years ago. No amount of money would get her to turn on my family."

"All right. However, you must agree, to throw a premiere party last minute isn't ideal."

"My mother can be impulsive and we all just have to be along for the ride. But I'm still really confused. If they aren't going to come at you through this book, then what?"

"That's the million-dollar question and I wish I had the answer. All I know is they are planning something. We need to be prepared." He took her chin with his thumb and forefinger. Needing to feel her lips against his, he took her mouth in hot kiss.

She clutched his shirt.

He thought she was going to push him away, but instead, she twirled and twisted her tongue around his in a wild motion. He groaned. "Does this mean you forgive me for not telling you about Marcus?"

"Only if you help me get rid of my hangover."

"And how do you expect me to do that?" he asked.

"By giving me an orgasm." She straddled him. Pulling off her shirt, she cupped her breasts, rolling her nipples between her fingers and thumbs.

He swallowed. Hard. "I have a few minutes before I need to head into work." He gripped her hips while enjoying the show. "I'm going to have to close tonight."

"So that means you won't be home until three in the morning."

"Pretty much." He batted her hand away and took her nipple into his mouth.

She moaned, arching her back and cupping his head. "Keep that up, I might be here waiting."

He lifted his gaze. "I hope so." Shifting to the other breast, he rolled her to her back. He dotted kisses down her tight stomach, tugging her panties to her ankles. "I know you want to visit with your family, but I'd feel better if you stayed here."

She reached down and grabbed him by the chin. "I can't over the weekend. I have to stay with my brother and my parents."

"I understand." He tossed her undergarments across the room. Standing at the edge of the bed, he removed his clothing as quickly as possible. "However, I want you to promise me you won't go near The Heritage Inn."

"Can we stop talking?"

He growled, lowering himself to the mattress, wrapping his arms around her sweet body, losing himself in her gentle touch.

Everything about her made him want to be a different man. To forget his past and everything he'd been running from, even though all the ugliness of it followed him to the most wonderful place in the world.

When he was with Brandi, none of that mattered. In the short time he'd known her, she'd fundamentally changed the way he viewed life.

For years, he believed all he needed was his brothers. They were his lifeline. They still were. He couldn't imagine what it would be like to have ventured into civilian life without them.

However, letting Brandi in and opening up to her had shown him that something had been missing from his life. He'd never thought he'd been capable of love. That he could ever trust a woman, in part because of Roxy, but also because the idea of sharing anything with anyone outside of his immediate family gave him anxiety.

Holding her in her arms, kissing her, and the idea that it could end, made his pulse increase with fear.

"Yes. Nelson, yes," she whispered, digging her fingers into his shoulder blades as he thrust himself deep.

Desperately, she ground her hips. Her climax took hold of him like a death grip.

His orgasm mixed with hers like a blender exploding. His vision blurred and his lungs burned.

"If makeup sex is going to be like that, we should fight more often," she said with a raspy breath.

He rolled to his side, pulling her tight to his chest, and laughed. "As good as that was, I'd prefer not to argue."

"You're no fun."

"Say that again, and I'll torture you after work."

"Is that a promise?" She glanced up and smiled.

"You're going to be the death of me." He kissed her forehead. "I have to head in. Call me if you need me."

"Actually, I need to set up a meeting with your chef and also bring Jared over to discuss security."

"I'll set something up for both," he said. "Probably tomorrow."

She kissed the center of his chest. "You're the best."

He slipped from the bed and found his jeans. "Listen. Even though I signed the contract and read the book, I'd like to keep that as quiet as possible."

"I don't have to file it yet. We're still in revise and resubmit."

"Please try to avoid Marcus."

"I have no intention of meeting with him. Not unless you think it's the right way to go. I'll either be here, my brother's, or at Blue Moon."

Bending over, he cupped the back of her neck and

kissed her one last time. "Promise me if you hear from him, you'll let me know."

"Wow. I'm not used to this overprotective side of yours."

He pulled his shirt over his head. "I know you're teasing me, but Marcus is—"

"Nelson. Go to work."

Brandi set a tray of cheese and crackers out on the table in the middle of the gazebo.

"Are you sure Nelson won't care that we're all here?" Tonya asked.

"I sent him a text, letting him know. He responded with a thumbs-up." Brandi felt bad she was the only one drinking alcohol. But Tiki and her sisters, Tonya and Tayla, had all had babies within a week of each other.

"Thank him for us," Tiki said. "I haven't been out of my house since Maddie was born." She rested her hand on the stroller next to her and gently rocked it.

"The only thing I've done is make a run to the store for diapers." Tayla grabbed her boobs. "I forgot to wear those pad things under my bra and some kid started crying and next thing I knew, I was leaking breast milk everywhere."

Tiki and Tonya burst out laughing.

"I hate it when that happens," Tonya managed.

Brandi couldn't relate, but ever since her sister-in-law had given birth, her biological desire for children had been tickling the back of her brain. Having a family had been something she'd always wanted. She just wasn't in much of a hurry. Her goal had been to prove to her father she could run the company so her brother could follow his dreams.

Then she'd figure out her love life.

Well, Lake had published one book and was on his way to a collaboration with his wife and a second solo book. And he had a daughter. His life was exactly where he wanted it.

Now it was her turn.

Only, she'd managed to fall for a guy who was as emotionally unavailable as a turnip.

"Do you want children?" Tonya asked as she lifted her fussy baby into her arms and stood.

"Someday." Brandi nibbled on some cheese and poured herself a large glass of wine.

"I take it since we're here at Nelson's place, you and he are somewhat of an item." Tayla had a warm, inviting smile. Much like both of her sisters.

Ever since Lake had fallen in love with and married Tiki, Brandi had gotten to know Tiki's sisters. Most of the time when she'd come to visit, they would all get together. Tiki was tight with her family and they welcomed all the Grants with open arms.

"We are," Brandi admitted. "But with all that's

going on with my mom's movie premiere, I don't want that public."

"My sisters won't breathe a word. They've seen firsthand what the media can do." Tiki reached out and squeezed Brandi's forearm. "But we have to know, what's he really like?"

"Yeah. I mean, he's always so sweet," Tayla said. "He's got a killer smile and greets almost everyone when they come into the restaurant. He's kind and charismatic. But outside of that, no one ever sees him."

"Lake has had a beer with him a few times." Brandi didn't want to sit around a fire and gossip about her boyfriend.

Boyfriend.

It felt strange to think that about Nelson.

When she'd walked away from him and tried to rekindle things with Ethan, all she could think about was what Nelson might be doing and who he was doing it with. Flashes of jealousy would fill her heart. That's when she knew she had to see him again.

The moment she'd laid eyes on Nelson, her pulse soared.

"That's not the same as male bonding," Tiki said. "Nelson has gotten friendly with a lot of people, but he hasn't become friends with anyone. If you're going to be dating Nelson, Lake wants to get to know him better. Have him over for dinner. Maybe double date."

So much had happened in a short period of time. Her relationship with Nelson had gone from zero to sixty in days and she didn't trust that it was because he wanted the same thing as she did. She worried that the stress of having Marcus around, and worrying about if Marcus wanted to hurt Nelson, pushed him into protection mode.

If that was the case, as soon as the threat was over, things would cool down and he might find himself pushing her away.

A reality she needed to face now.

"Lake doesn't need me to make a new friend," Brandi said.

"What my sister is trying to ask, but failing miserably, is she wants to know what's really going on with you and Nelson." Tonya set her little one back in the stroller and patted its back. "Tiki has never been a gossip and it's been like pulling teeth on why here when we got the invite to come over. We get you want your privacy protected. We've all experienced breaches in trust. If you don't want to talk about it, we get it, but you look like you've swallowed an entire bushel of lemons. Something is bothering you. This is a safe place."

"I'm under a lot of stress." She followed the stern light of a boat as it buzzed up the shoreline. "I don't want Lake to worry about anything with the business. I'm dealing with my mother and her movie premiere. It's just a lot."

"It's more than that." Tiki tilted her head. "Something changed between last weekend and today. You've been distant with both of us and Lake is taking it personally."

Now she understood Nelson's position.

She couldn't talk about the situation with Marcus. That would be beyond breaking a confidence. She couldn't even discuss a lot of it with Lake. Not anymore. Too many lines had been crossed.

But she could express her feelings about Nelson.

Girl talk.

When was the last time she'd done that?

Never. She didn't have women friends.

Hell, she wasn't sure she had friends. Not in the true sense of the word. When she went out, it was with co-workers or friends of the family. When she'd been dating Ethan, they hung out with his friends.

"Honestly, I have no idea what I'm doing." Brandi leaned over and adjusted the flame of the fire before topping off her wine. She lifted her cell to see if there were any messages from Nelson.

None.

He'd been quiet most of the day.

Nothing to report. That should be good news, but part of her wanted a random text now and again.

Wasn't that what boyfriends did?

"What do you mean?" Tayla asked.

"Taking an on-again, off-again fling into an exclusive long-distance relationship. It's a crazy decision.

On both our parts. He works nutty hours and is never going to visit me in the city. Once my dad retires, it's going to be harder for me to get away."

"I'm going to say something that is going to piss you off." Tiki shifted. "You've wanted your father's approval forever. You needed him to treat you like Lake's equal. It drove you crazy that he didn't believe you were as capable as Lake. But what you want for your future has changed."

"I am the future of Grant Publishing," Brandi said, but her tone lacked conviction.

"What about your cousin, Edward?" Tiki asked. "He's young, he's passionate, and he's got blind ambition."

Brandi used to think she had ambition, but since her father had turned over half the reins, she realized her drive had been more about proving her ability than wanting to be the face of the company.

"Where do you see yourself in five years?" Tayla asked. "Is it career? Family? Both?"

"I want both," Brandi admitted. "For years I believed that would always happen in the city. I'd find someone like-minded. Maybe in the business, but definitely not an author."

"But that didn't happen," Tonya said. "You found Nelson."

"Are you in love with him?" Tayla asked.

Brandi choked on a cracker. She pounded her chest, cleared her throat, and took a sip of wine. "I care about him, but it's way too soon to be tossing around that word."

"I don't believe that." Tiki lowered her chin. "Maybe it's not the right time to say it, but those feelings can happen quickly. It can sneak up on you and before you know it, you've fallen head over heels."

"I totally agree with that statement," Tayla said.

"I was in love with Foster for years. It took us being best friends before we could express our feelings." Tonya lifted her child out of the stroller. She leaned back, brought her baby to her chest, pulled up her shirt, and began feeding.

Brandi's heart melted.

That was definitely something she wanted and she wasn't getting any younger.

"Long distance isn't an easy way to have a relationship," Brandi said. "Especially when two people are committed to their careers."

"Are you kidding me," Tiki said. "That's lame."

"I'm with my sister." Tayla shook her head. "Gael and I made it work in the beginning."

"So did Lake and I." Tiki arched a brow. "You've even said you wouldn't mind having a place up here and working remotely occasionally. And I would bet that has something to do with Nelson."

Her cell buzzed. She lifted it and narrowed her gaze. "Nelson is on his way home with Lake."

"Why?" Tiki leaned over. "Is something wrong?"

She reread the text.

Nelson: *Don't want to alarm you, but Marcus is in a boat not far from my dock. I'll be home in fifteen. Lake is with me. Stacey Tanner is patrolling nearby, keeping an eye on things.*

Her heart thumped like a jackhammer in her throat. Knowing a state trooper was close by did make her feel better, but why would Marcus be spying on Nelson's house, when he was at work?

Either Marcus intended on breaking in or he was watching her, and that made her want to climb right out of her skin.

She clutched her cell to her chest.

"Foster is texting me, telling me he's on his way," Tonya said.

"I just heard from Gael." Tayla scooted to the edge of her chair, waving her cell. "He mentioned he was under strict orders not to leave until Nelson or Reese arrived."

Tonya masterfully held her baby in one arm and her cell in her free hand, tapping at the screen. "Foster was given similar instructions. When I asked for information, I got, *Babe, I'm driving. See you soon.*"

"Brandi? What's going on?" Tiki asked. "And don't lie to me."

"I'm not sure, exactly." That was the truth.

"I don't believe you." Tiki glared.

"Hang on." She stood, taking five large steps toward the house. She pulled up Nelson's contact information. It rang once.

"Hey. I'm ten minutes away. Are you okay?" Nelson asked.

"No. I'm freaking the fuck out and so are Tiki and her sisters. They want answers and I don't know what to tell them."

"I'm probably overreacting to the situation, but I thought it was better if their husbands picked them up. Your brother was at the restaurant with me when Reese told me what was going on. Reese hopped in a patrol car with Jared. They left at the same time I did, but they are driving like there's no speed limit."

"That still doesn't give me any suggestions for how to handle Tiki and her sisters."

"You can tell them that someone from my past has paid me a visit and I'm being paranoid," he said a little too calmly. "I've filled Lake in on what I can."

"Should they be concerned for their safety?"

"No. Marcus wants me, but that means he could come through you to do it."

"That means he could come at my brother and his family, which means, yes, they all should be worried." She turned and faced her friends.

Friends.

That was new territory, and one that she would protect.

10

Nelson hadn't held too many babies in his life. It wasn't that he didn't like the cute little buggers, because he did. He simply hadn't been exposed to them often.

"Are you sure you want her while she's screaming?" Lake asked.

"According to your sister, all she ever does is cry." Nelson took the infant into his arms and gently rocked back and forth. "Hey there, princess. You've got a big set of lungs, don't you?" He pressed his lips on her temple and inhaled Maddie's fresh baby scent. Lifting her to his shoulder, he kept his cheek against hers and patted her back, humming softly.

Maddie continued to cry, but her wails weren't as powerful.

"You're a natural." Lake pointed to the fridge. "Mind if I snag a beer?"

"Help yourself and get me one while you're at it." Nelson continued to sway, bouncing a little more aggressively. But what really seemed to do the trick was making noise in Maddie's ear.

Lake twisted off the caps to two bottles and set one on the counter. He tilted his head. "Her eyelids are growing heavy. Whatever you're doing, you will have to teach us."

"I'm humming against the side of her face."

"Are you kidding me?" Lake rubbed the back of his neck. "We've tried so many different things, including singing, dancing, everything short of letting Maddie cry it out. We both think she's too young."

"I know nothing about babies except they smell like a little piece of heaven."

Lake smiled like a proud father. "Even with her colic—which is what the doctor says she has—she's precious." He took his daughter from Nelson and placed her in the tiny portable bassinet, ensuring she was swaddled tightly. "Our pediatrician says she'll outgrow this in a couple of months. My mother told me that my sister and I were colicky for almost three months. But one day, we stopped."

"I'm sure she'll do the same thing."

"The lack of sleep is getting to Tiki."

Nelson took his beer and sat on one of the stools at the counter in the kitchen. He glanced over his shoulder. Brandi and Tiki were huddled in front of the fireplace in the living room. He lifted his cell off the counter.

Reese confirmed that Marcus and his crew were back at The Heritage Inn.

Stacey had given them a ticket for not having their lights on while fishing. They tried to get out of it by flexing their military background, but Stacey held her ground. They were lucky they had all the proper fishing licenses as well as having the boat equipped with the required safety gear.

Marcus accused her of police harassment and warned her that he'd be taking it up with her boss.

She handed him his ticket and Jared's business card.

Nelson found that to be insanely funny. The more time he spent with Jared and all his state troopers, the more he liked them.

"I'm sorry to be adding to your stress," Nelson said. "Your family has a lot going on. My drama is the last thing you need."

"Unfortunately, we're kind of used to this." Lake tapped his bottle against Nelson's.

"I wish I knew what the hell Marcus really wanted."

"Maybe all he wants to do is mess with your head." Lake leaned against the counter.

"He's succeeding in that department, but based on what I read in that bullshit manuscript, he wants revenge."

"Do you think that storyline is a precursor for what is to come? Because if it is, that's not only fucked up, but then I'd push my mom to change the venue of the premiere."

"Murdering me wouldn't be smart." Nelson rubbed the back of his neck. "Although, the female lead got away with it and she was pretty ingenious in how she did it."

"I must admit, that idea was pretty creative and plausible, which scares me for you now that I know some of what he wrote is true. Not to mention learning that he didn't attend that conference puts a different spin on things."

"Putting it in writing and then doing it would be the dumbest thing ever and Marcus isn't stupid. If his plan is for me to be six feet under, why would he write about it and send it to someone I've been seeing? However, whatever his plan is, it won't be good." Nelson waved his finger. "You're going to need to explain to me how he ended up submitting to her if he never went to that writer's convention in the first place."

"Long story short, she couldn't take the pitches, so everyone was told they could submit. He must have heard that from someone and took a calculated risk that she'd open every submission," Lake said.

"When was the conference?"

"About four months ago."

"It takes that long to get a manuscript read at your company?" Nelson had been told that publishing could be slow, but that seemed a bit long for a writer to wait in the world of self-publishing. Not that he knew anything about it.

"She didn't get the manuscript until four weeks ago. Her assistant read it and thought it had merit. Brandi sent him a revise and resubmit with our suggestions on what we feel would be a better book. He's still pushing to speak to her face-to-face. If all this wasn't happening, that would still be a huge red flag, and at this point, we'd reject just because we don't need high-maintenance authors. Maybe she should take that meeting with—"

"Absolutely not." Nelson shook his head. "I don't want her anywhere near him."

"You didn't let me finish." Lake set his beverage on the counter. "I would go with her and we'd do it at your restaurant. We'd make sure that someone from Jared's office was there. Maybe someone off duty."

"I can guarantee you that Marcus won't like you being part of the meeting." Nelson lowered his chin. "This is about manipulating and controlling whatever his endgame is."

"Up until recently, the line he submitted to was mine. The transition to making Brandi head of everything took time. We needed our writers and our staff to trust the process. However, it hasn't been announced in any major publishing forum. That won't happen until after my mother's movie comes out. He doesn't know that I don't have anything to do with the military thriller line. Even if he did, my last name is still Grant. When my father retires, I will still own half that company. Just because my sister will run the day-to-day, that doesn't mean she and I won't be making all the decisions together. We can approach the meeting as I pushed her into listening to his ideas. That I wanted the meeting."

Nelson lifted his beer and guzzled it down. The alcohol couldn't hit his bloodstream fast enough. He had to admit that everything Lake said made sense, except for one thing. "He'll know it's a setup and he'll be full of more crap. I don't want more games. I need to know what the hell his real plan is, but he's one step ahead of me."

"I don't pretend to understand your world. I've never served in the military, but I have been involved in a few scandals. I've been manipulated by some crazy-ass people in my day, and the one thing I've learned from those experiences is sometimes you have to play their game in order to come out on top."

Nelson stood, inching closer to the living room. He planted his hands on his hips and let out a slow breath, doing his best to calm his nerves. "When my brothers and I bought Blue Moon, it was meant to be a new beginning for us. For Phoenix, it gave him the excuse to leave the military after an injury that was going to force him out of being in the field. Maverick had already had one foot out the door. His girlfriend wasn't a fan of the three of us being in business together, whether it be back in North Carolina or up here. In the end, she told him it was either her or us."

"That's a terrible position to put anyone in."

"Maverick didn't even blink," Nelson said. "But it did fundamentally change him."

"I'm sure it has."

"Living here has been good for all of us. We're putting down roots, something we've never done." Nelson turned. "I care about your sister."

"I can see that." Lake leaned to the right. "I'm butting in where I don't belong, but I sense that you don't know if you want this relationship or not."

Nelson chuckled. "Neither one of us can be completely committed to it. We've each got one foot in and one foot ready to run."

"I appreciate your honesty."

Nelson strolled back to the kitchen island. "I'll agree to the meeting with Marcus on two conditions."

"What are they?"

"It takes place in my restaurant and you let me bug the table so I can listen in."

Lake nodded. "We'll set it up."

"Set what up?" Brandi strolled into the kitchen.

Tiki was one step behind, although she stopped at the bassinet, taking a quick peek inside.

"Your brother talked me into letting you and him

meet with Marcus." Nelson reached across the counter. He gripped the red wine bottle and poured it into Brandi's glass. He climbed up on the stool and rested his elbow on the island.

"Let me? Wrong choice of words." She patted the center of his chest before easing in between his legs. "And why do I want my big brother tagging along? Don't you think that will tip him off we're up to something?"

"It wouldn't be the first time you and I met with an author together," Lake said.

Nelson wrapped an arm around Brandi's waist, letting his hand fall on her hip. He hadn't shown affection for a woman in front of a group in a long time. He thought it would feel awkward, especially around Lake and his wife.

But it didn't.

"What would seem weird is if I attended the meeting," Nelson said. "Besides, I'm guessing he wants to see how I react and what I might overhear. He's been out in the open with everything he's done until tonight. He needs to gather more intel, but he needs to do it without us watching. It's why he didn't eat at my restaurant tonight and why he rented a boat from a dock in the village and not Reese." He rested his chin on her shoulder. "I'm sure Stacey giving him a hard time pissed him off. That's going to put him on the defensive and it might force him to show his hand."

"Or it might make him hostile," Lake said.

"That is a concern, which is why I want the table bugged and I want at least one trooper in the building."

Lake glanced at his watch. "It's almost ten. Let's send this email first thing in the morning and try to get this meeting set up tomorrow."

"I'll draft it tonight and shoot it off by seven tomorrow," Brandi said. "I bet I hear from him within an hour after that."

In the background, little Maddie began to fuss. Tiki went to her side and patted her back.

"Explain to me what this revise and resubmit plan has in it." Nelson needed to understand what Brandi put out there so he could control the narrative.

"I've given him alternative plot lines that are more in line with what we're willing to publish." Brandi shifted, putting her arm over his shoulder. "It doesn't change the plot, but it does change where and how we would market it."

"And it does change the ending," Lake said.

Tiki continued to attend to her child. "Think of it as *it takes a village,*" Tiki said. "When Brandi edited my book, there were a few changes she wanted and one of them I fought her a little on."

"A little?" Brandi laughed. "You argued with me for three days until you finally came to the realization that my idea was what was best for the book."

"But it wasn't the first one you came at me with,"

Brandi said. "It was like the fifth one that we brainstormed together."

"However, this was after she was already under contract. Marcus isn't a signed author," Lake said. "So, in this scenario, we simply tell him what we liked, where it falls short, and some ideas that would give him a higher chance of being bought. It's no guarantee that we would sign him."

"Okay, so during this meeting, maybe you could suggest a few things that might hit too close to home." Nelson knew this would be playing with fire, but sometimes that was the only way to get the job done.

"What do you mean?" Brandi narrowed her eyes.

"Marcus twisted what happened to me during that mission. What happened to my men. To the SEAL team. He wants to paint this picture that I'm responsible for Seth's death as well as Roxy's miscarriage. Why don't you suggest that the female lead have the baby and that the father is the man she was having the affair with. Let it play out that way."

"We were toying with that idea anyway," Lake said. "Another idea was if the villain wanted the husband dead, but the husband was only MIA (missing in action), but comes back—"

"Oh. I've got a better idea." Tiki lifted a crying child into her arms. "Based on what I've heard, Nelson's character is the villain, right?"

"That's correct." Brandi nodded.

"If you're trying to push this guy Marcus' buttons,

why not make it a little more true to what happened, but twist it where it will hurt the most." Tiki cocked her head.

"What are you suggesting?" Nelson shifted.

"That we turn the tables and make the book about exactly what he's trying to hide," Tiki said.

"That actually might work," Lake said.

"If you both are thinking what I'm thinking, I agree." Brandi turned her head and bit down on her lip. "But it would mean putting a little bit of your truth out there."

"What truth?" Nelson asked.

"We suggest to Marcus that he rewrite the story so that Roxy's character goes to Nelson's character with the sole purpose of getting pregnant. She's successful and it's Nelson's character that's left to die."

"That would change everything about the novel," Nelson said.

"It's not what I suggested in my original letter." Brandi ran a hand through her hair. "But we could approach this meeting as we've chatted and we believe we have a better way to take the story."

"If he's going to push his version of the truth, it will piss him off, especially if you're adamant that his manuscript isn't worth publishing as written." While Nelson didn't like the idea of putting his girlfriend in a situation where Marcus could become hostile, he had to admit, this was a good idea.

"Brandi and I can run with this idea," Lake said.

"I hate to state the obvious, but we better get this little one home." Tiki bounced up and down. "She's been an angel tonight, but I don't want to press our luck."

"Are you coming with us? Or staying here?" Lake asked.

Brandi glanced over her shoulder. "Are you kicking me out?"

"Never." Nelson kissed her nose.

"Don't forget to copy me." Lake collected the bassinet and all the other baby items.

Nelson walked to their vehicle, checking the surroundings. Jared had promised that both local and state would be driving by his place, as well as Lake's house. "Text me when you get home."

"Take care of my sister." Lake stretched out his arm.

"You have my word." Nelson stood in the driveway and watched Lake pull out onto Assembly Point. Turning, he strolled down the path. He locked the front door and headed back to the kitchen where he found Brandi sitting at the island with her laptop open. "I take it you're already constructing that email to Marcus."

"I'm going to schedule now so we don't have to worry about it."

"Good idea." He snagged a water bottle from the fridge. "Are you almost done?"

She closed the computer. "Yes," she said with a heavy sigh.

"What's the matter?"

"I hate to admit it, but I'm scared."

He took her into his arms. "So am I."

11

"I hate waiting." Brandi checked her watch. "He's fifteen minutes late." She lifted her water glass and sipped before glancing around the restaurant. "Nelson is always punctual. Actually, he's always early. He says that's a military trait. I would think Marcus is the same way."

"I'm sure he is," Lake said. "Nelson mentioned Marcus might play games with us, so I'm also not surprised."

"He's probably sneaking around, doing recon—that's what the military would call it." She sucked in a deep breath. "I'm worried he might know Tristan Reid's a trooper." It took all the discipline in the world not to look over her shoulder at Tristan. He'd planted himself at the bar with a friend. She had no idea who he was or if he was a trooper too. It didn't matter.

The bases had been covered.

Somewhere at the table, Nelson had planted a bug. She didn't know where it was, and she didn't want to know.

"Here he comes," Lake said.

Her heart crawled up her esophagus and landed in the center of her throat. Every time it beat, it closed off her airways and she thought she would suffocate to death.

Dramatic? Perhaps.

It was as if she were about to land in the climactic scene of one of the books she edited.

"I'm so sorry. I had to take care of some family business." Marcus strolled up to the table, stretching out his arm. "You must be Lake Grant. It's a pleasure to meet you."

"You as well," Lake said. "Please, have a seat." He waved his hand in the air and nodded in the direction of Veronica. "What would you like to drink?"

"Whatever you're having is fine." Marcus leaned over the table and clasped his hands.

"Two beers on tap and a glass of rose," Lake said. "Along with a sampler of appetizers to start."

"I'll bring the drinks right over and put in the food order." Veronica nodded.

"You didn't have to order any food on my account," Marcus said. "I thought I mentioned that my time is limited and I can't stay too long."

Brandi squeezed her fingers together. He had not stated anything of the sort. Not to mention it was unprofessional, considering he'd been pushing to have a discussion with her face-to-face.

"Then we should get down to business," Lake said.

A brief moment of silence passed while Veronica placed the drinks on the table before scurrying away.

"I have to admit that I was surprised Brandi called this meeting." Marcus lifted his beer. "She'd been so adamant that I go back to the drawing board on my manuscript and that I make all those adjustments before there was any chance of a dialogue."

"My brother thought—since you're in the area—it would be a good idea to sit down and chat about the direction of the rewrite and resubmit." Brandi folded her hands in her lap.

Nelson thought playing it as though she wasn't thrilled with her brother meddling in her acquisitions would be best. It wouldn't be hard to do that since she was on edge. She could also draw on all the times she and her brother disagreed on a book and how it should be edited or marketed.

"I've read your manuscript and while I agree with my sister that some changes need to be made, I wanted to hear what your thoughts were about her ideas and if you had any of your own." Lake had an incredibly diplomatic way about him, and Brandi's father had always told her that she needed to be more like him if she was going to have total control of the company.

She'd spent the better part of the last year learning to have a softer edge when it came to handling situations like these. However, if this was an actual manuscript they were considering, they wouldn't be having this meeting.

She also believed that authors needed to develop a thick skin. She got tired of having to be tactful in her assessment of their work, especially new writers. It was one thing to be professional. It wasn't like she had any intention of hurting a person's feelings. What she did want to do was make the book better for readers and ultimately, bring in the sales numbers.

If authors felt their version of the novel was better than her suggestions, they needed to be able to express that in a way that sold the editor. Half the time it wasn't the plot that was the problem, but the execution.

In Marcus' case, it was both if you took out what he'd done to Nelson. His ideas were cliché at best. She'd seen a million of those manuscripts come across her desk. Normally, they were rejected. However, every once in a while, the execution—or the twists of the same old idea—were so impressive, she wanted to read more or have the author give it another go.

This was the game they were playing with Marcus. At least on the surface.

"I'm curious as to why you found the ending so intolerable." Marcus leaned back, his demeanor relaxed and slightly arrogant. "I get it's disturbing, but it's meant to be psychological. It was meant to leave the reader gobsmacked and wondering if there would be more, which I'd like to make this a series." He smiled like a kid running into a candy store and being told he could spend his entire allowance.

"It's really hard to write the antihero," Lake said. "And I'll be honest, this didn't pull it off." He held up his hand. "I do like the concept of having a rough around the edges hero who doesn't do things by the book, especially if we can make him a hero in more than one novel. You won't do it if you make him an accessory to murder."

"I've read what Brandi thinks I should do with the rewrites," Marcus said. "What do you suggest?"

"I take it you don't appreciate my sister's ideas." Lake sipped his beverage.

Brandi opened her mouth to protest how much she hated it when anyone discussed her as if she wasn't even at the table, but Veronica showed up with their appetizers.

That was probably a good thing. She needed to keep her cool and antagonizing Marcus wasn't the way to do that.

She filled a plate with a couple of chicken wings, a few onion rings, and one quesadilla. She wasn't overly hungry, but she braced herself for wanting to eat her feelings. Even though this wasn't a real business meeting, it was going to suck to have to listen to her awesome editorial opinion be torn apart by an asshole who wanted to mess with her boyfriend's mental state. "Whenever you get the chance, can I get another glass of rose?"

Lake arched a brow.

She ignored it as she took a nice hearty gulp of her adult beverage. Once a week her mother went out with her two best friends. They called themselves *the ladies who lunch*. And with that title, they allowed themselves two glasses of wine.

If they could do it, so could she.

She scanned the bar area, looking for Nelson, but found no sight of him, because he was up in his office, listening.

Her feelings for him had intensified to a level she hadn't anticipated so quickly, making her want to return to New York City's safety net. She could hide in the sea of people. The constant movement and noise allowed her to blend in and never really be seen or heard. It was a luxury that many didn't understand.

But it could also be a lonely existence, and the thought of returning to it tightened her chest.

She was falling hard for Nelson and there was no turning that boat around.

"It's not that I don't value Brandi's opinion." Marcus pushed his plate aside and turned his attention to her. "I was so impressed with your lecture at the conference and how you handled the questions that came at you during the panel discussions."

Liar. He hadn't attended, but he could have managed to purchase the audio recordings, or perhaps he's just a bold asshole and she should catch him in the act.

"I knew of all the editors there; you were the one I wanted to submit to," Marcus said.

"What in my workshop struck a chord with you?" She picked up her fork and knife, slicing through her quesadilla and stuffing a large piece into her mouth.

His answer should be amusing.

"It wasn't any one thing in particular, but I will say I enjoyed how you were more specific about wanting something different. Giving examples of how to twist things and make characters unique. Based on what I heard you say, I did some rewriting before submitting."

Shit. She said that kind of shit in interviews all the time. If anyone googled her, they could find it in a blog. Nothing new there. "I do like the way you did a lot of things. However, you pushed too far at the end. It's a lot to ask the reader to go on a dark journey and root for the bad guy."

"But is she really a bad person? Or a good person put in a shitty situation and ends up—"

"I love that scenario," Brandi interrupted Marcus. "Tossing everything we can at a character is awesome. But there has to be a glimmer of redemption. Revenge as a motive is hard to pull off. The reader needs something tangible. You need to define it.

Murder is the goal. In your case, the wife's motive is she believes the antagonist purposely let her husband die because he wanted her to himself, but he has no idea about the baby or that it could be his. It's too cliché."

"That is where I do agree with my sister." Lake waved a French fry before dunking it in ketchup. "But I think I might have a better solution than what's been suggested so far."

"I'm anxiously waiting to hear it, because I'll be honest, I wasn't loving Brandi's direction." Marcus shrugged. "I'm sorry. No offense."

"None taken." She smiled. "It's your book and you have to do what you think is best. Mine are but suggestions. If you send me back something else and the execution is spectacular, we'll buy it. If it's not, maybe another publisher will feel differently." Standard verbiage. It wasn't bullshit either. Some writers walked away feeling like they got some editorial crap that was given to everyone. Well, sometimes it was, but it was still a truthful answer.

Lake leaned forward and laced his fingers together as if he were excited. "I believe you have the wrong hero and antagonist."

"I'm not following." Marcus scowled.

"Your antagonist should be your hero and your female lead, Rose, should be your villain. She should be the mastermind. She should come after Anderson, who cares for her but doesn't want to be with her anymore, especially since she's married to someone else. She lies, works him good. Does whatever it takes to seduce him. She needs to be pregnant, and Anderson looks similar to her husband. Same build. Same eye color. Same hair color."

"I don't know about this," Marcus said, shaking his head. "I feel like this has been done before."

"Every storyline has been done to death." Lake leaned back. "But I'm suggesting that Anderson is the one who's left behind and the husband and Rose go on as if nothing happened."

"The beauty of this plot twist is the husband doesn't know anything. Rose's brother was in on it. He made sure Anderson was left for dead. But Anderson comes back to seek his revenge. This is the kind of broken hero readers can get behind." Brandi swallowed her beating heart. Her raging pulse wasn't out of excitement, but more out of disgust. She hated acting as though any of this was okay.

The worst part was, this wasn't a horrible storyline.

"There are a few ways you could write this, but in the end, the hero could find a new love interest. He could be a fallen hero in the sense that the military would see him as a traitor for some reason. There could be so many reasons he can't just come out and say what happened. Plus, he won't know the baby is his until after it's born. So many turning points. So much conflict. The ending could be a tender moment between baby and father," Brandi said.

"Do it right, and this could be a series with a new hero and heroine working together to solve all sorts of different injustices in the military and political arena." Lake raised his glass. "Write that story and do it well, I can guarantee you we'll buy it."

Marcus' normally arrogant expression had been replaced with a tight lip and a narrow stare. He lifted his hand and rubbed his jaw with his thumb and forefinger. "That's an interesting idea."

"Again, this is your story. You need to tell it your way. These are suggestions." Brandi lifted her finger. "However, I can't say this enough. If you want Grant Publishing to be your publisher, I'd consider making some serious changes."

"Take your time. Think about everything we've said. There is no timeline on resubmitting." Lake continued to nibble on the food.

Veronica brought Brandi's second glass of wine just in the nick of time. If she had to sit here any longer without alcohol, she'd lose her freaking mind.

"You've given me a ton to mull over and I appreciate your time." Marcus pressed his hands on the table. "My sister is here. She got a new job about two months ago in New York City where her boyfriend lives. I had no idea it was for your mother's public relations firm."

"Excuse me?" Lake stood.

"Roxy, my sister, works for Keller P.R. and she's here with her boss, Leslie, for the movie premiere. I couldn't believe when she called me a couple of days ago to tell me she was coming up. I haven't seen her since she moved." He glanced toward the door, then smiled and waved. "I'm sorry, but I've got to run." He held out his hand. "It was so nice to meet you, Lake."

"You as well." Lake nodded.

"I'll be working on that manuscript and sending it back as soon as possible." Marcus pushed his chair in, turned, and practically skipped like a child toward a woman with long blond hair wearing a pair of jeans, black boots, and a dark-gray sweater.

Brandi glanced over her shoulder and up the stairs. She couldn't see through the windows, but she knew Nelson was up there listening, which couldn't have gone over well.

"Did Mom or Dad say anything to you about new hires at the PR firm?" Lake asked.

"Nope and you know how Mom gets. She trusts only Leslie. In the last twelve years, she's never worked with anyone else." Her cell buzzed in her purse. She leaned over and lifted it. "It's Nelson."

Nelson: *Veronica is coming over. I need you to vacate the table so she can remove the bug and put it wherever Marcus is going to sit.*

Brandi: *Where do want us to go? And did you hear all that?*

Nelson: *Sit at the bar or out on the patio. Just don't* *leave without me. And yeah, I heard it. I'll be down in a minute. They want a reaction out of me; I might as well give them one.*

Brandi: *Don't do anything crazy.*

Nelson: *Jared's in the parking lot. Tristan's at the bar. Maverick and Phoenix are wandering the premises. Nothing is going to happen.*

Brandi doubted that.

12

Nelson opened the office door and was greeted by Phoenix. "Thanks for coming up to the office." Nelson had texted both his brothers, asking for one of them to take over listening in on Marcus. He hadn't explained anything about Roxy, but she wouldn't have gone unnoticed. His siblings all knew who she was, and he was sure they were concerned about why she'd joined her brother.

"It might be a good idea for you to stay here with me," Phoenix said. "You're a hothead when it comes to Roxy. Besides, I want the details on what you heard. I only got bits and pieces and most of it didn't make sense."

"I need to get downstairs." Nelson cocked his head and gave his brother that look that said, *get the fuck out of my way, or I'll move you.* He adjusted his cell and the recording app so they could hear the conversation Marcus and Roxy were having, but so far, it was all benign. It was almost as if they knew someone was listening. Or at least suspected and were being careful.

That's what Nelson would have done.

Phoenix held up his hands. "All right. But before you go down there, do you even have a plan? Or are you going to go right to attack mode and give them the advantage, because I bet she's only here to rattle your cage."

"No, actually, she works for the company that does all the PR and publicity for Brandi's mom." Nelson wiggled his fingers and relaxed his shoulders. He took in a slow, calculated breath. Everything about Marcus' and Roxy's presence was to upset Nelson. What he didn't know was what they expected him to do. Or what they were going to do as an endgame.

That was still a huge issue and he hadn't learned anything from Marcus' meeting with Brandi and Lake, other than Marcus' demeanor had changed when the truth about what his sister had done had been tossed in his face.

That was proof enough to Nelson that Marcus knew all about Roxy's plan to get pregnant, even if it was something he learned afterward. Nelson still didn't understand why she'd chosen him when having a one-night stand would have been easier.

There was something they were missing. Something that tied this all up nice and neat. He'd always suspected Marcus and his team had been up to something illegal out in the field, but he had no idea what, or if it included Seth and his SEAL team.

Nelson upped the volume, lifting it to his ear. Roxy mentioned something about her boyfriend. His name was Ken Vander and he was a plastic surgeon in Manhattan and he was going to some convention for the weekend.

"That's an interesting and potentially dangerous twist." Phoenix glanced down the steps. "When your mission went in front of the review board, Dad always said that Marcus was gunning for you. He had it on good authority that some of the things Marcus, Chuck, Josh, and Tyler testified to didn't ring true. That the investigator found discrepancies in their stories."

"Joe and Tony told mostly the same story, but at the time of the ambush, they'd been separated from their team. It wasn't until Marcus found me that they had been able to find their way back," Nelson said.

"You've always thought there was something bigger at play during that mission."

"The entire thing was a clusterfuck from beginning to end." Nelson kept the cell between him and his brother. "The intel I had gotten was shit. I was ambushed two miles from where the SEAL team had been held. Marcus' team was ambushed and they came from the other direction."

"That's not unheard of if the enemy intercepted your call," Phoenix said. "Seth's team had been killed between fifteen minutes to an hour before your arrival based on the after-action report and what was gathered from enemy information."

"That's the belief." Nelson rubbed his side. The sound of gunfire filled his brain. The memory of his men shouting, then screaming, and finally, the sound of silence. Nelson had no idea if the quiet had been because he'd lost consciousness, or because of the death that had surrounded him, but it didn't matter.

The enemy had destroyed them because they knew they were coming.

The question had always been, how had that been possible?

"The enemy knew we were coming. The timing was too perfect, but it took so long for my memories to go from hazy to somewhat clear."

"But the review board didn't find you at fault, even though Marcus testified that he didn't get your distress call. That it came from the nearby civilian town."

"That's bullshit. But I can't prove it because my Satcoms were damaged and I couldn't connect to even terrestrial communications. All I had was short-term radio frequency and a prayer." Nelson had gone over this a dozen times with his brothers. He didn't have a problem doing it all again. He had a tickle in the back of his mind. There was a missing link and he needed to find it, fast.

"When you were cleared and given a medal, there

was nothing else for the military to investigate. It was case closed. At least to the public," Phoenix said. "Only Dad keeps telling us that he believes there is an active investigation regarding both the deaths of the SEAL team and the ambush of yours."

"I put a call into Dad. I'm hoping he can return it sometime today," Nelson said.

"I'm surprised the only Snow we've seen so far is Maverick," Roxy said.

"Nelson's here. I'm sure of it," Marcus said. "He'll show his face soon enough. Patience. You need to learn to have some. We might not be in this situation if you exercised it a couple of years ago."

"Don't put this on me," Roxy said. "My actions have nothing to do with the way things went down. Besides, I told you what my plan was, and you only told me to make sure Seth didn't find out until after he was deployed. I made sure of that."

"You have a selective memory because I also told you that you were playing with fire and to just let me handle your husband. But no, you had to go pull fucking Nelson into this."

"The military did that when they sent him to save Seth."

"That's exactly what we wanted. Now be quiet. We shouldn't be talking about this here," Marcus said.

"What the hell?" Phoenix mumbled. "Sounds like you were collateral damage in something that had to do with Seth."

"I told you something fucked up went down on that mission." Nelson rubbed the back of his neck. "The information coming to us about the status of the SEAL team was iffy at best. The ambush was too perfect. I don't remember what happened after that. I only have what Marcus and his team told me."

"And every one of those fuckers survived." Phoenix tilted his head.

"Joe and Tony aren't here. That's a little suspect, don't you think?"

Phoenix nodded. "It took a long time for the man who took my spot after I was injured to become tight with the rest of my team. He's a brother now, but I'm included in everything they do."

"I'm thinking we should reach out to them and see what they have to say."

"I don't disagree," Phoenix said.

"I need to get down there. I don't want Marcus or Roxy to think I'm hiding. I also want to check on Brandi. I know that wasn't easy for her." Nelson handed Phoenix his cell. "I won't have any way to communicate, so come get me if you need to. And text Mom and Dad with all this. We need them to pull some strings and find out as much as they can about any investigation that has occurred or is happening about that mission."

"On it," Phoenix said. "Watch your back and don't let either one of them bait you. We've got something to go on now."

Nelson swallowed the bitter taste in his mouth. For years after their breakup, he had a soft spot for Roxy.

He only wanted what was best for her, and when she'd come to him that night, he'd been taken for a ride.

The few times he'd seen her after that, she had the ability to get under his skin like no other, mostly because she lied right to his face and then had the audacity to call him the liar.

What he didn't understand was how what she'd done to him was connected to whatever illegal activity Marcus and his crew had been doing.

And was Seth involved?

Or had he found out something and they needed to get rid of him?

A million more questions ran through his brain.

He did his best to keep his emotions in check as he strolled through the restaurant, nodding and smiling to all the regular customers. He and his brothers had built a steady clientele and he had no intention of letting his past destroy it.

Nor was he about to let Roxy and Marcus ruin what he had going with Brandi. His feelings for Brandi were a great source of confusion. He cared deeply and he didn't want it to end.

As a matter of fact, he saw a future for the first time in a long while. One that included a family—something he hadn't thought about in over a decade. The idea had come from nowhere. He'd been drinking his coffee and staring at her from across the kitchen, and a vision of her sharing his home in a forever way popped into his head.

The feeling of a baby in his arms, touching his skin, had been overwhelming. Love had eased into his heart and he didn't even know it.

Slowly, he passed by the opening of the main dining room. He turned his head, his gaze catching Marcus'.

Bile filled Nelson's throat. He swallowed, but the nasty taste lingered.

Roxy looked in his direction. The corners of her mouth turned upward, but it wasn't a warm and welcoming smile that an old friend would share. This had a sinister feel to the expression.

Nelson paused for a moment, contemplating whether or not he should engage right away.

Out of the corner of his eye, he noticed Maverick approaching from the bar area. "Phoenix told me what he heard. Do you want me to go in there with you?"

"I'm not going to go say hello just yet."

Maverick crinkled his forehead and nose. "If you don't go over there, they will come to you once you walk away. It's not like you can avoid this. You've got to play the game."

"I'm playing all right." Nelson nodded. "But I don't have to play by their rules." He sidestepped his brother. "Time to shake things up." He locked gazes with Brandi as he rounded the corner onto the patio. His heart pounded. He hated that she had a front-row seat to the ugliness that Marcus and his sister brought to his front doorstep. He resented the hell out of the fact that they used Brandi and her family to get to him and for what?

A question that couldn't be as simple as to shame Nelson. Or even destroy his business.

The only real explanation that made sense was finishing what they had started.

But what was that, exactly?

"Roxy just bolted out of her chair," Maverick whispered.

"Good. I want her to witness this," Nelson said. What he was about to do was a calculated risk, but one that could pay off in his favor.

If Brandi and her brother didn't kill him first.

"Do you really want to flaunt your relationship with Brandi in their face?" Maverick muttered.

"They already know, so why hide it."

"To protect her," Maverick said.

"I can't do that if I don't put them on the defensive, forcing them to show their animosity toward me." Nelson squared his shoulders. "You know I'm right."

"I can't argue that point," Maverick said.

"Hang close, I might need you."

Brandi sat at the table closest to the water and sipped a glass of wine, while Lake held a beer with his legs stretched out and crossed at the ankles. They both looked relaxed, but he knew they weren't.

They were anything but and Nelson could tell by

the way Brandi tapped her fingernails against the chair.

A nervous habit.

She glanced over her shoulder and smiled.

"Hey," he said, taking her hand and tugging her to a standing position. "You did real good. Both of you." He cupped the side of her face, running his thumb under her cheek. "Lake, I'm sorry if what I'm about to do makes you uncomfortable and please don't hit me. At least not right here."

Brandi's lips parted. Her big blue-green eyes grew wider. "What are you going—"

He hushed her with a passionate kiss. One that belonged in private. His tongue slipped into her mouth on a search-and-destroy mission. He heaved her to his chest, wrapping his arms tight around her firm body. He'd started the romantic moment by counting to twenty. He thought he'd end it then, figuring that was long enough to prove his point.

He'd managed to get to three and then got lost in the moment.

Someone cleared their throat in the background and reluctantly, he broke lip contact.

"Well, that was nice," Brandi managed with red cheeks.

"I thought so." His heart filled with emotions he had no label for. Ever since the mission that changed his life, he'd been running from his past. Running from the pain. Trying to hide from it as best he could, not allowing any real feelings to surface.

Now that Marcus and Roxy were standing directly behind him, he realized she was always going to be part of who he was no matter where he went or what he did.

He'd accepted his role in what happened, but he would no longer allow anyone else to blame him for doing his job, and that's exactly what he'd done. He also wasn't about to let the past walk away with his future.

Not anymore.

"Care to explain why you did that when we were planning on keeping things quiet for a while?" She rested her hands on his shoulders, keeping her focus on him, not anything—or anyone—else. Brandi Grant being in a relationship with anyone would be news. Bigger news that it's the owner of Blue Moon, the establishment holding the main event.

That made him wonder why Marcus hadn't outed them yet. That had to be part of the grand plan. Perhaps he wanted to create a scandal on premiere night. That made perfect sense.

"I will later, but for now, please follow my lead," he whispered and turned. Time to face the firing squad.

Roxy stood five feet away, her brother next to her on the water side. Neither one of them looked shocked at the public display of affection, but both had a perplexed expression with their tight jaws and narrowed stares.

For the last week, Nelson had been on defense, constantly reacting to Marcus and his buddies. This was the first time that Nelson took the bull by the horns.

"Hello, Nelson," Roxy said. "I can't believe you walked right past me—made eye contact—and didn't acknowledge me." She pushed out her hip and planted a hand on it. She had a smug smirk and looked him up and down like he was a lowly human who didn't belong anywhere. Then her gaze shifted to Brandi and she did the same thing.

Talk about irritating.

Maverick had taken a step back, almost blending in with the wall. He'd stand there, waiting until he either needed to intervene, or until the encounter was over.

"Sorry," Nelson said. "I was busy in my office on calls all morning and I wanted to see my girlfriend before anyone else." These next few words were not going to go over well, but he didn't care. "Especially you." That last comment should be enough to piss Roxy off.

Roxy glared. "I'll ignore that last comment." She lifted her chin and stretched out her arm. "I know *he's* not going to introduce us, but I'm Roxy Baxter, Marcus' sister. I work for Leslie, your mother's publicist. I'm so happy for Phoebe and can't wait to see the movie. I'm really looking forward to meeting her."

A litany of questions filled Nelson's brain. He made a mental note of every single one, but he'd start with the most obvious. "You haven't met Phoebe yet? That's strange if you're working on her PR."

"Not really," Lake said. "My mother is particular and doesn't trust anyone other than Leslie. She doesn't care that Leslie has assistants, or who they are; she doesn't want them around. Only Leslie. She's been like that for years."

Roxy pursed her lips. "I was brought here this weekend to work. Phoebe knows I'm here."

"Roxy Baxter?" Brandi lifted her index finger to her lip. "I don't remember seeing your name on the guest list." She turned to Lake. "Did you?"

"No." Lake shook his head. "Mom and Leslie gave us the updated one this morning, too."

Roxy's jaw twitched. She always did that when she was pissed. She waved her hand. "I'm sure it was an oversight. I'm here to help make sure everything runs smoothly." She shrugged. "I hear you're going to buy my brother's book. That's so exciting."

"Did you actually make Marcus an offer today?" Nelson asked with a hint of humor in his voice.

"Not yet. We need him to make some changes before that can happen." Brandi took Nelson's hand and squeezed.

He rubbed his thumb over her soft skin.

"I'm surprised you didn't tell me that you and my editor were an item when I mentioned to you that I was meeting with Brandi last weekend. You had to have seen us together," Marcus said. "Why would you keep that from me? You knew how excited I was about the whole thing."

"Brandi doesn't discuss her clients' work with me. Not until after it's about to hit the shelves. And even then, she doesn't go into details." Nelson had to admit, the game was getting good. Even if he wasn't getting information, he was enjoying making them uncomfortable. "If I had mentioned something, she might have felt like I was trying to sway her one way or the other." He arched a brow. "Considering our history, I thought it was best she didn't know. I wouldn't want to be accused of asking her to reject you if she chose not to buy your book."

Marcus widened his stance, as if he were ready for a fight. "Are you trying to change her mind now that it's more real because Lake is involved?"

"Lake and Brandi have always worked side by side." Nelson did his best to bite back a smile. "So don't worry. I don't want to be involved in whatever business you have with Grant Publishing. That's between you, Lake, and Brandi. But I don't like keeping secrets from my girl, so this morning I told her that we knew each other in the military."

"Why this morning?" Marcus held up his hands. "I'm just trying to understand what changed. It seems strange that you'd keep it a secret one day, and when Roxy shows up the next day, you get territorial. Not to mention it was rude."

Nelson understood that Marcus was doing two things.

Fishing for information.

And doing his damnedest not to show his hand.

Only he wasn't doing a very good job with the latter.

"There is no love lost between me and Roxy." Nelson held Marcus' gaze. "However, my walking past your table has nothing to do with anything other than wanting to see Brandi. I'm sorry that you took it any other way."

"What does it matter?" Maverick asked. "Brandi's private life is separate from her professional one. So is Nelson's and if he wants to take a moment—even at his own place of business—to spend some time with his lady, he can and we should all respect that. Something you have no clue about."

"Wow. You still enjoy sticking your nose where it doesn't belong." Marcus jerked his chin. "I'm starting to worry that any misunderstandings or disagreements that I—or my sister—have had with Nelson could end up playing a role in my book deal."

"We're professionals at Grant Publishing," Brandi said. "That would never happen."

"Does that mean you know that Nelson and I used to be a couple," Roxy said with a stupid grin on her face. It was like she'd exposed some deep, dark secret. "Unfortunately, it didn't end well."

Brandi leaned closer. "Actually, he told me about it." She squeezed his biceps.

"I'm sure he didn't give you the entire picture." Roxy shifted her gaze between Nelson and Brandi. "But I want you to know that what happened between us won't affect my job when it comes to making sure this event goes off without a hitch."

"Since I'm the one in charge, I know it won't." Brandi glanced at her watch. "Lake, you need to get going."

"We won't keep you any longer," Marcus said. "I'm sure our lunch will be served any second now, and then I've got to go meet the boys and Roxy has work to do." Marcus took his sister by the elbow. "Thanks again for meeting with me. My head is spinning with all the possibilities." He turned and guided Roxy back toward the main dining room.

"I remembered to keep my brother from hitting that man," Maverick said under his breath. "But I wanted to throttle both he and his bitch of a sister."

"We rattled their nerves. That's good." Nelson palmed Brandi's cheek. "I'm sorry, but we need to talk about the fact Roxy is working for your mom's publicist and how that changes this weekend."

"I did see a Roxy Baxter on the list as Leslie's errand girl. Not her new assistant. But she is allowed to attend the premiere," Brandi said.

"When you asked me to host this party, you mentioned that it was your mother's and her publicist's idea." Nelson dropped his arm to his side. "I wonder if Roxy might have planted that idea in her boss' mind."

"That sounds like a real possibility and I can see how my mom would run with it." Lake nodded. "I've already texted both my parents. My dad's in meetings right now, but he said he'll call in about forty minutes. They are taking a private charter tomorrow, but something tells me they might show up tonight."

"That might not be a bad idea. Especially if they can do it quietly." Nelson looped his arm over Brandi's shoulders. "Maverick, do think you and Phoenix can hold things down here while we go back to my place to discuss the next steps and call the Grants?"

"I'll keep an eye on those two," Maverick said. "We've got a full staff today, so Phoenix and I can sneak out if we need to."

"Perfect. Thanks, man. And let me know if you hear from your mom and dad." Marcus and Roxy could fuck with Nelson's life, but no way in hell was he going to let them mess with anyone in Brandi's family.

13

"Nelson?" Brandi strolled down the steps to the lower dock, careful not to spill an oversized glass of Pinot Noir. "Are you down here?" She glanced at the brand-new twenty-eight-foot cabin cruiser with twin inboard-outboard engine. From what she could tell, he'd barely used it. He also had a rowboat and a small fishing boat parked under the sundeck.

Both were brand new as well, and both were equally untouched.

She'd always known that Nelson hid from something painful within the confines of his restaurant. That work had become his only way to cope with whatever haunted his soul. Now that she'd gotten to know him better and understood what he was running from, she wished he could settle his mind and heart a little and enjoy his life.

He deserved it.

"Yup." He sat on one of the Adirondack chairs, his legs stretched out and his ankles crossed. He swirled a glass of red wine and stared at the setting sun. "I needed some fresh air."

"My parents are going to head over in about ten minutes." She eased into the big chair and sighed.

He chuckled. "This is not how I expected to meet your parents for the first time."

"You've met them a couple of times already."

"Yeah. But not as your boyfriend. That kind of changes things."

"What are you worried about?" She kicked off her shoes and tucked her feet up under her butt. "The situation? Or how they will respond to us dating?"

"Both." He lifted his glass. The settling sunrays caught the rim. His blue eyes sparkled in the evening sky. "However, my first concern is the security at the restaurant."

"Jared and my mom's team have that covered." She reached out and rested her hand on his thigh, massaging gently.

"My military background dictates that I worry about it. Not to mention the whole Marcus, Roxy situation." He set his drink on the dock and rested his hand over hers, rubbing his thumb tenderly over her skin. "If my past wasn't colliding with your family, it would be another day at the office. But because I'm sure he's here to harm me and possibly my brothers, you and anyone in your family could be collateral damage." He kissed the back of her hand.

"Couldn't be as simple as he wants to expose the affair and how he believes your actions killed Seth?"

"If they want to bring out my one-night stand with a married woman, I can handle it. If they want to dig up rumors and drag my name through the mud, I'll endure it. Worst thing that can happen is me and my brothers have to start over again."

"That would suck."

He smiled. "It would. But it wouldn't be the end of the world and depending on how everyone in this town takes it, it might even blow over. Unfortunately, I don't think Marcus has spent all this time planning and writing a fake novel in hopes of ruining my reputation. That's too much of a crapshoot and he's not a gambler. Not in that sense of the word."

Brandi had been rolling over all the possible outcomes in her mind for hours. She'd listened to Lake and Nelson discuss the book and what was true and false. They'd reviewed the information Leslie had sent regarding Roxy's employment and how that came about. What really got under her skin was that Roxy had been the one to suggest to Leslie that a premiere in Lake George might be a great publicity stunt for both the movie and Grant Publishing and make it easier for Lake and Tiki to attend.

Leslie had her reservations about moving the

venue, but she saw the merits and brought it to Brandi's mom, who jumped all over it.

That didn't surprise Brandi. "Do you really believe he's dangerous? I mean, he saved your life."

"Only because he was obligated to."

Brandi's heart dropped to the bottom of her gut. Her breath got stuck in the center of her chest. "What do you mean by that?"

"He was the commander of a six-man A-Team. You've met three of the men who served with him and were there when he found me."

"So, there were two others on that mission."

Nelson nodded. "Joe and Tony."

"Do you find it strange that they aren't here celebrating with the rest of the team?" Brandi asked.

"What's off is the fact that Marcus lied about it." Nelson rubbed his temples. "He told me they had family obligations and that's why they weren't attending Chuck's bachelor weekend."

"I take it you found out the real reason."

"I had a buddy of mine do some checking and Joe and Tony asked for a transfer shortly after the mission in question."

"You didn't know that?" She set her wine aside and took his hand.

"I was in a hospital in Germany for a month. The only visitors I was allowed were my immediate family and a few key military personnel. They allowed Marcus to visit me once." Nelson dropped his head back and closed his eyes. "For the longest time, I thought it had been a bad dream."

"What did he say to you?"

"He whispered in my ear to regain my strength because when the time was right, he was coming for me. That it wasn't a threat. It was a promise. That if he could have left me out there to die, he would have."

The oxygen in Brandi's lungs turned to thick smoke. "When did you realize that actually happened?"

"I was heavily drugged at the time," he said. "I was in and out of consciousness and my memories of the time were more than fuzzy. But I heard the words clear as day. I opened my eyes, and he smiled this sinister grin and tapped my broken ribs. It wasn't hard, but enough for me to feel the physical pain."

"That's cruel."

"He's not a nice man." Nelson blinked, turning his head. "I wanted to believe that I was reliving what happened in the field. The crushing pain. The inability to take a full breath." He placed his hand over his chest. "After Marcus left that day, I started having flashbacks to the moment that Marcus brought me back from the dead. I thought I was crazy, but my therapist believes that there's a real possibility that my memories could be real."

"And what is it that is haunting you?" Tears burned her eyes.

"It was almost like being jerked awake from a nightmare. I gasped for breath, only I felt like I was drowning. The first thing I saw was Marcus. He leaned over and told me it would have been easier for everyone if I had stayed dead. He said it would be okay if I gave up the fight and lay down like a dog. Or something like that."

Her heart broke into a million pieces. No wonder Nelson had packed up his life and hid from his past. She stood, straddled Nelson's lap, and cupped his cheeks. "That's horrible."

"I never stopped fighting to live. But I did do what I needed to do to put the past in my rearview mirror and forget all about Marcus, Roxy, and that part of my life. Only, they found me and are now threatening people I've come to care about. I'm not going to take that sitting down." He ran his hands down her back, squeezing her ass. "The only thing I did wrong was sleep with Roxy when she was still married to Seth."

"She told you she was separated."

"That doesn't make what I did right." He arched a brow. "I didn't care about her anymore. I didn't even like her that much. I have no good reason for what I did except I wanted sex and she was familiar."

"You had a long-term relationship with her at one time. It makes sense for people to fall back on that." Brandi leaned in and brushed her lips over his mouth. "You're not the only who's done that." She cocked her head. "Or do I need to remind you about Ethan?"

"That's such a bad comparison." He chuckled. "You weren't using him for sex because you had me."

She had to admit, Nelson had a point. She narrowed her stare. "Perhaps not. But I went back to someone I had known, not because I loved him, but because it was comfortable."

"Versus someone who's new and you didn't know well at all. Someone who scared you."

"Please. You don't frighten me."

"I believe the idea of us did, or you wouldn't have gone back to him." He brushed back a few strands of hair that had blown across her face. "I didn't realize how much you mattered to me until that short break we took, but being in a meaningful relationship does make me want to run."

"Why?" Her heart pushed to her throat.

"Part of it is because of what happened with Roxy. And the other part is knowing that Marcus was always one step behind me. It's like I've been waiting for death to catch me."

"Don't talk like that." She poked him in the chest.

He took her hand and kissed it. "I don't mean it literally."

"You better not." She shifted her body, swinging her leg to the side and wrapping her arms around his shoulders.

"I've never voiced this to anyone other than my brothers, but I think there was something else going down during that mission. Something that either my team got in the way of, intercepted, or stopped from happening. Marcus doesn't want payback for Seth's death. Or Roxy's miscarriage."

"You don't believe that's reason enough."

"It is, but since he didn't use it against me when he could have, I feel like I'm missing something." He held her tighter. "I'm hoping my parents with their contacts can help."

"You haven't heard from them?"

"Only that they're working on it and will call as soon as they have something."

Her cell dinged. She pulled it from her back pocket. "My parents just pulled into the driveway."

He groaned, dropping his forehead to her shoulder. "All of a sudden, I feel like I'm seventeen again and I'm about to get grilled about my intentions."

"Oh, my dad will give you a hard time." She laughed. "And I'll have fun watching you sweat."

Nelson hadn't dated most women long enough to entertain the idea that he should meet their parents. The last time it happened had to have been a good four years ago and it successfully ended that short-lived relationship. Not because the encounter didn't go well, but because he realized the girl wanted more than he was willing to give.

He ducked his head in the fridge and pulled out

some cheese, pepperoni, and grapes to go with the wine he'd already opened. He arranged the food on the tray and found some chocolate to go on the side. Entertaining had never been his strong suit. Kind of funny, considering he'd bought a restaurant and learned the business by trial and error.

Sucking in a deep breath, he headed toward the family room for the grand introduction. He'd given Brandi and her parents a few moments alone together. He thought they would enjoy some time with their daughter, and they could get caught up from her perspective.

"Here he is." Brandi jumped to her feet from the leather chair she'd been sitting in across from her parents. "Mom, Dad, you remember Nelson Snow from Blue Moon."

He set the platter on the coffee table. Rubbing his hand on his thigh, he stretched out his arm. "It's a pleasure to see you both again."

Chandler Grant pushed to a standing position from his perch on the sofa, taking his hand in a firm shake.

"You have a lovely home," Phoebe said as she smoothed down the front of her slacks.

"Thank you. I'm just sorry about the drama that my past is causing your business and family."

"We're more concerned about what Marcus' intentions with you are at the moment." Chandler leaned over and fixed himself a small plate before sitting back down. "I took the time to skim through the submission, and if any of that is based in reality, it's quite disturbing."

"There are some truths in the manuscript." Nelson appreciated Chandler's desire to get right down to business.

"I understand that the history of it all mixes fiction and true life, but it's the ending that I'm worried about, if it's meant to be a warning or threat of some kind." Chandler shifted his focus between Nelson and his daughter. "We've discussed what it would take to postpone the premiere party or even move it."

"I'm not opposed to either," Nelson said. "It would take me out of the equation when it comes to your family's celebration."

"Let me ask you this. Do you honestly believe Marcus and his friends are dangerous?" Chandler held up his hand. "As in, will they hurt my daughter, my wife, or my son and his family?"

A slow burn filled Nelson's chest. It was like a fire broke out inside his body and engulfed his heart. "The only thing I know for sure is he wants to hurt me. How he plans on doing that is up in the air. But because Brandi is part of my life, then he could get to me through her, or any of you."

"All this because of something that happened between you and his sister years ago?" Phoebe asked. "I'm sorry if I seem out of the loop on this, but I don't understand this level of revenge for what has been described to me."

"I believe this goes much deeper than Roxy," Nelson said.

"Mom, Dad, so much of this Nelson can't talk about. The details of the mission and what he did in the military. It's all still classified," Brandi said.

"Sweetheart, we understand that and we're not asking him to." Chandler leaned forward. "I can't go to the studio and ask them to change or postpone anything that they've dumped a ton of money into unless we've got something real to go on and right now, we don't even have a tangible threat."

Nelson lifted his glass and stood, strolling to the picture window. He stared out at the water, his gaze scanning for threats in the area. He knew good people were keeping an eye on Marcus and his crew. He'd get a text the second anyone lost contact with any of them. "I've always felt like I was missing a big piece of the puzzle on the day Roxy's husband died and my team was ambushed." He lifted his wine to his lips and sipped. "My dad is a general in the Army and my mom works for the Department of Defense. They are both using their contacts to investigate the failed missions and what could really be driving Marcus today." He turned. "There is this tickle in the back of my brain that is telling me that I was supposed to be a fall guy for something and it didn't work out that way."

"We have three days," Chandler said. "I'm comfortable with the security we have and all the extra measures we're taking with the exception of one thing."

"Roxy," Phoebe said. "I've never met the young woman. Leslie said she was hired by the firm a few months ago, but Leslie brought her onto her team when Roxy came up with some bold ideas and good ones too."

"Roxy's a smart girl." Nelson inched across the room, standing behind Brandi's chair. "She graduated top of her class. She's always done well in anything she's ever tried."

"She asked for an extra ticket," Phoebe said. "I've asked Leslie to deny the request."

"That's for the best." Nelson rested his hand on Brandi's shoulder. "We've put Marcus on the defensive and I can tell by his responses today that we've rattled him a bit. But it's hard to figure out his plan until I can nail down his motivation and goal for wanting to destroy me."

"And that brings us back to the fact that you don't believe it's what happened between you and his sister," Chandler said matter-of-factly.

"I've run that time in my life over in mind a dozen times." Nelson shook his head. "Marcus and I were never all that close. We butted heads most of our lives, but when I first dated his sister, we at least got along. When Roxy and I ended things, Marcus and I went back to being combative. But I don't understand the level of animosity. That's why I believe there's something that I don't know. Something that happened out there during that mission."

"What's the likelihood that you'll get the information you need to figure it out?" Chandler asked.

Nelson let out a long breath. "The military is secretive for a reason. I've never questioned it, until now." He pulled his cell out of his back pocket, quickly glancing at the screen.

No messages.

He waved the phone in the air. "My dad promised he'd reach out to me tonight by midnight no matter what he had."

"Where do your parents live?" Phoebe asked.

"They're in DC now. Been there for about four years. They both work at the Pentagon."

"If they want to get away for the weekend, we can get them tickets." Phoebe smiled. "We'd love to meet them."

"My mom's a huge fan." Nelson was grateful for the shift toward a more normal conversation. "She's seen you on Broadway twice."

"Really? That's so sweet," Phoebe said. "What are the chances they could get away to come up for the premiere? We could send a charter plane to get them."

Nelson swallowed the lump in his throat. "That's very kind of you, but—"

"Please. Extend the invite. If they can make it, great. If not, we'll have to set up another time for all of us to get together. I'm always down to meet a fan, but more importantly, the parents of the man who has turned my daughter's head," Phoebe said.

It took a lot to make Nelson blush, but that statement brought heat to his cheeks.

"Lake tells us that this thing with the two of you has been going on longer than we've known." Chandler leaned back, crossing his legs. "And here I thought she was coming up to spend time with her brother and sister-in-law."

"That's what she told us." Phoebe sat a little taller, resting her hands in her lap. "All these weekends and she had a secret boyfriend."

"I was a little taken aback when we showed up at Lake's this afternoon and none of my daughter's possessions were there." Chandler arched a brow.

"Either she's ashamed of us—or him," Phoebe said.

"Mom, I get Dad with his pokes, but you? Really?" Brandi sighed. "I asked you not to do this."

"Sweetheart, we can't help ourselves," Chandler said. "We knew Lake and Tiki weren't the only reason you kept dashing off. We've been waiting patiently for you to tell us. Now we get to have our fun."

"Do it with me, not Nelson." Brandi folded her arms.

"It's okay." Nelson sat on the edge of the seat and

pried her hand out from the tight hold she had around her middle. He understood her frustration. He'd listened from the other room when she begged them not to pick on him—or her—for that matter. "I think we deserve a little razzing. I know I'm going to get it from my parents."

"What do they know about the two of you?" Chandler lowered his chin.

"Less than you." Nelson saw no reason to lie. "Unless my brothers have been feeding them intel, which is entirely possible."

"I have to ask." Chandler leaned forward and snagged a couple of crackers with cheese. "What are your intentions with my baby girl?"

"Stop it." Brandi bolted upright.

"What?" Chandler lifted his hands. "It's a legitimate question for a dad to ask any man who's sleeping with his daughter."

Nelson pounded his chest. He'd been warned that her parents didn't often have a filter.

"Dad, that was rude." Brandi shook her head.

"What's wrong with your father wanting to know more about your bed partner?" Phoebe asked.

"You people are so embarrassing. This is why I don't bring boyfriends home," Brandi mumbled.

"So, this relationship *is* serious," Chandler said.

"It's new territory for me." Nelson closed the gap and put his arm around her waist. "Whatever happened to watching me squirm?" he whispered.

She tilted her head and glared.

He couldn't help it and laughed.

"I don't see how you can find any of this amusing." Brandi looped her hand through his arm. "Are we done with the jokes?"

"For now." Chandler glanced at his watch. "We should get going. Mom wants to spend more time with Maddie before she turns into a holy terror and starts screaming again."

"I hear Nelson is a bit of a baby whisperer." Phoebe stood, taking her husband's hand.

"He is really good with her," Brandi said.

"All I did was hum in her ear." For the second time that night, Nelson found himself feeling comfortable in a situation that would normally make him want to run, and run fast. However, he wanted to embrace a world he never thought he wanted. Every minute he spent with Brandi, he fell harder for her and he'd stopped fighting it.

"Well, that trick of yours has made their life so much quieter," Chandler said. "And hopefully will allow us some sleep. Otherwise, you might have yourself two more houseguests."

"You're always welcome." Nelson made his way to the front door. "I'll let you know the moment I hear any news about the Marcus situation."

"I appreciate that." Chandler squeezed his shoulder. "Take care of my baby girl."

"I will, sir." Nelson stood in the doorway with a

protective arm around Brandi and watched her parents climb into their rental and drive away. "I like your parents."

"The feeling is obviously mutual." She leaned against the door and they locked gazes. "What are we doing?"

He jerked his head back. "What do you mean?"

"We just made this thing between us very real."

"Because it wasn't before?"

"I didn't mean it like that. But we went from zero to sixty in the blink of an eye."

He took her into his arms and kissed her nose. "I thought we'd already had this conversation and the fact that we care about each other and want to see where this takes us."

"I know. But taking a leap of faith is one thing. Falling head over heels for you is something else." She rested her hands on his shoulders. "I'm in over my head."

He took her chin with his thumb and forefinger. His heart thumped in the center of this throat. "I'm so far gone for you I can't see straight." He took her mouth in a hot, passionate kiss. Never before in his life had he felt this connected to another person outside of his immediate family.

Outside of his brothers and parents, he didn't trust people. That ended the day his military career ended. Deep down, he knew something had gone sideways and he'd been lied to by the people he worked with; he just didn't know who or why.

It had hardened him, but Brandi changed everything.

She loved as fiercely as she fought for what was right. She was kind, smart, and could hold her own in any situation. She made him want all the things he either thought he couldn't have or shouldn't want.

He lifted her by the thighs, and she straddled his waist as he stumbled to the bedroom. He grappled with her clothing, needing to feel her skin under his fingertips.

He was desperate to be inside her, giving her pleasure. His muscles shook as he entered her body, thrusting hard.

Her nails dug into his back and her legs wrapped tightly around his waist, encouraging him to forgo all the nuances of lovemaking. Everything about this encounter was raw with the sole purpose of getting lost in the sex.

But there was an underlying sense of love that couldn't be denied.

It was so profound that when her climax slammed into his, he was momentarily blinded. His lungs burned as he tried to take in a deep breath and couldn't. Holding her against his chest, he welcomed what being in love meant.

Now he had to muster the courage to say the words.

14

Nelson rolled to the side and reached for his cell.

"What time is it?" Brandi brushed the hair from her face. "Who's calling?"

"My dad and it's five in the morning." He kissed her temple. "Go back to sleep." He swung his legs to the side of bed and found his pants. "Hey, Dad," he whispered.

"Sorry, it's so early."

"No worries." Nelson tiptoed to the patio and sat on the chaise lounge. He put the cell on speaker and stretched out his legs while he checked his messages.

Since the last time he checked, Reese had texted once, letting him know that Marcus had a boat reserved for six.

That made it harder for everyone to keep track of him.

"What did you find out?" Nelson asked.

"Why don't you come open the front door, let me in, and I'll tell you all about it."

"Shit." Nelson jumped to his feet. "You're here?"

"Both Mom and I just pulled into your driveway."

"Give me two minutes to get dressed." He tapped the red button and raced back through the sliding glass door, tripping over the track. "Fuck." He grabbed his foot and hobbled to the bed, landing on the corner of the mattress.

"What's wrong?" Brandi asked.

"My parents decided to grace us with their presence."

"Excuse me?" Brandi sat up, clutching the sheet across her naked body. Her blue-green eyes widened with a combination of fear and shock. "You mean they are in the house?"

"They will be when I go unlock the door." He glanced at his big toe. No damage, except to his ego. He stood, ignoring the sting.

"This is going to be an awkward first meeting."

"You can stay in here and hide if you'd like."

She tossed a pillow at his ass. "Do they even know about us?"

He lowered his chin. "Brandi, of course they know." He headed toward the hallway. "They don't know that I'm in love with you and that will come as a shock."

"What did you just say?" Brandi's voice went up an octave.

He gripped the doorknob and blinked. Had he just declared his love out loud? Slowly, he turned.

She sat on the bed, holding the sheet in one hand and covering her mouth with the other.

He wiggled his finger. "That is not how I wanted to say that for the first time."

"If you were trying to knock my socks off, it worked."

"I'm sorry that came out so flippant." His parents would have to wait another minute. He'd take hell for it, but he was used to that. Sitting on the edge of the bed, he took Brandi's hand. "Too soon?"

"Last night I freaked out about how we went from having fun to being a couple overnight, but not because I don't want it. I worry it's not what you want long term, and we've talked about that."

"I've been running from my past for so long that I never thought about what would happen if a future landed in my lap. All the women I've dated eventually found me to be cold and distant."

"You're not the easiest man to get to know."

He laughed. "My mother has always said I'm like an onion who doesn't want to have my layers peeled."

"That's a good way of putting it." She palmed his cheek. "You should go let them in."

"Don't you have something you want to say to me first?"

She brushed her lips over his mouth. "I can't think of anything."

"Are you kidding me? You're seriously going to leave me hanging?"

Her smile was as wide as the great state of Texas. She took his hand and placed it over the center of her chest. "My heart is pounding."

"Why? Are you afraid?"

"Yes," she whispered. "I've been in love before, but never anything like this."

Ding-dong.

"I better go let my parents in. Take your time coming down."

"I won't be too long."

Trying not to trip on anything, he raced through the house and yanked open the front door. "Sorry. I didn't mean to leave you standing outside." He hugged his mother and gave her a kiss on the cheek.

His dad took him in for a fatherly embrace.

His mom looked him up and down. "With how long you took, the least you could have done was put on a shirt."

Shit. "Let's go in the kitchen and put on a pot of coffee."

"We brought breakfast." His father held up a bag.

Immediately, his nostrils filled with the rich scents of fried eggs, bacon, and melting cheese over an everything bagel.

His favorite.

"Where's Brandi? Isn't she here?" his mother asked. "We brought extra for her, although I wasn't sure what she liked." She set a briefcase on the counter.

"She's getting dressed. She'll be out in a bit." Nelson filled the pot with water and went about making an extra strong pot. Both his parents loved their coffee black and strong as hell.

"Maybe she can bring you a shirt." His mom tilted her head.

"I've got one in the laundry room." Lucky for him, he'd done a load yesterday and they were folded on top of the dryer in the next room. He quickly snagged one, pulling it over his head.

"Before we get into Marcus and some things we've learned, we want to know how serious things are with this lady friend of yours," his father said.

"Both your brothers think this is the real deal."

"It is," Nelson admitted. "You'll like her."

"All we want for you is to be happy," his father said. "If Brandi brings you joy, then I'm sure we'll love her."

"What's her mom like?" His mother climbed up on the stool and leaned over, resting her chin in her hands.

"She's supersweet and they've invited both of you to the premiere party."

"That is so kind of them," his mom said.

"You can tell them we'd love to attend." His father

moved about the kitchen as if he lived there. It never bothered Nelson. These were his parents and they'd always made themselves at home. But all of a sudden, he became hyperaware that Brandi would be spending more and more time here and at some point, he wanted them to live together.

As scary as that thought was, it's the direction his life had taken.

Nelson took down four mugs, but only poured three, setting aside the last one for Brandi when she did decide to step from the master bedroom. He blew into the dark brew, which was a little stronger than he normally liked, and took a long sip. "You didn't come all the way up here to talk about Brandi, so what did you find out?"

"We did want to meet Brandi." His father unzipped the bag and pulled out a tablet. "And she could be part of why Marcus and Roxy are here."

"How so?"

"We'll get to that when she's in the same room so she can shed some light on the things we've found," his father said.

"No. You can tell me now, especially if you believe—"

"Don't get defensive." His mother raised her hand. "This isn't accusatory. There are some things we uncovered that she probably has no idea about. This is all a chain reaction leading up to this moment."

"Can Brandi be present when we go over every detail? Including the ones from the mission?" Nelson asked.

His parents glanced at each other like they used to when he'd been a teenager and they were deciding his punishment for being bad. They never even had to say a single word. They just knew what the other was thinking.

"She can." His dad held up a finger. "But she can't tell her parents or brother what we discuss. The only people who will be read in on this are your brothers and the state police."

"Jesus, Dad. I feel like you've totally ambushed me."

"I know and I'm sorry it had to be this way." His dad put out four plates around the kitchen table along with the necessary utensils. "Your brothers don't even know we're here yet."

"What the hell have you uncovered?" Nelson asked.

"Why don't you go get that girl of yours and we'll discuss everything we know." His mom took her mug and moved to the table. "Don't take too long or we'll assume one of two things."

"Do not put her through any harassment." He pushed from the counter and stared down his parents with the best version of his father's evil eye he could manage. "We went through enough of that last night. Besides, I'm not a child."

"No. You're a grown man." His father laughed. "But you'll always be our child and embarrassing you is our number one job."

"You've done a good job of that my entire life," Nelson mumbled.

Brandi held on to Nelson's hand with a death grip.

"Relax," he whispered.

"Right, because you're not twitching either."

"Not about you meeting my parents. Just about the fact they flew here because whatever they found out they felt the need to tell us in person." He pulled open the bedroom door and practically shoved her through it.

Taking in a long, slow breath, she did her damnedest to calm her nerves. She squared her shoulders and smiled, painfully aware she'd not had the chance to shower and didn't have a stitch of makeup on.

"This must be Brandi." With style and grace, his mom rose from her seat at the kitchen table. "I'm Dina and this is my husband, Louis."

"It's a pleasure to meet you both."

Nelson pulled out a chair and she settled into it, wondering if everyone could hear her heart thumping like a raging river smashing against the rocks. "My parents brought food."

"I'm starving." She helped herself to one of the egg sandwiches, hoping that picking at it would help calm her nerves.

"Why don't we get right down to business." Louis tapped his fingers on the tablet. "The first thing you both should know is that there has been an investigation into Nelson's mission and near death—"

"I did die, Dad."

"Yes, we're all very well aware of that fact," Dina said. "We don't like to be reminded of it."

"Anyway, the Army and Navy have been investigating the events leading up to Seth's SEAL team becoming compromised and subsequently captured and the events that followed. We've both been stonewalled every time I've asked or your mom has. That's standard because we're your parents." Louis pulled up a document with a top secret and confidential stamp.

"At one point, I was told that the case was wrapped up and all accounts had been fact-checked and the government's stance on the incident was bad intel and that you did nothing wrong," Dina said.

"I know I didn't." Nelson slammed his cup on the table. A splash of coffee flew over the rim and landed on his hand. "Fuck." He grabbed a napkin and cleaned himself off. "Sorry, Mom, but the way some people tried to spin what happened, making it sound like my decisions were reckless…"

"The good news is that the military knows you

acted appropriately based on the situation and the intel you were given." Louis turned the tablet toward Nelson.

Brandi leaned closer, resting her hand on his shoulder, doing her best to follow the conversation.

"What we didn't know until Mom pushed harder with her contacts is that the Army has an open investigation into Marcus," Louis said. "The Navy has been looking into a connection between Seth and this man."

Brandi's heart dropped to her toes. "That's Ethan."

Nelson jerked his head. "Your ex-boyfriend?"

She nodded. "I told you he was in the Navy."

"Did you know Seth Baxter?" Dina asked.

"I don't believe so." Brandi pulled the tablet closer, widening the picture on the screen. "Ethan did four years at the Naval Academy and then served two years after that. He didn't like it and didn't talk about it much other than he was grateful for the degree and the experience."

"He was at the Naval Academy at the same time as Seth," Louis said.

"What does that have to do with our current situation?" Nelson asked.

"Ethan's company is well known for data security."

"We use EMS Security for our data protection at Grant Publishing," Brandi said.

Dina leaned over the table and scrolled to another document. "The Department of Defense was in discussions with him a few years ago to safeguard military secrets and data. Two months before Seth's team was deployed on their last mission, I voted to pull the plug on the contract with EMS Security." Dina leaned back in her chair.

"Why?" Brandi asked.

"I'd been given information that Ethan was known for putting in backdoors in many of his programs. We can't have any of that bullshit going on when it comes to national security," Dina said.

"Where'd you get the information?" Brandi struggled to believe that Ethan would do something like that when it came to the government. However, she did know he'd done it with other companies. When questioned about it, his response was always the same.

He did it to protect the data. That only he and his team could find the backdoor and that in the event of a breach, they had a way of hacking back into the system.

It made sense when he explained it. But what the hell did she know?

"That's the interesting part." Louis stood, taking his mug with him as he casually strolled across the room.

"There was a committee looking into Ethan and every aspect of his life. It included you," Dina said. "Of course, that had no bearing on our decision. But what did was the source that came from inside the Navy, and I was not given the full information at the time."

Brandi rubbed her temples. Her brain filled with more questions than answers.

"Who was it and what did they say, exactly?" Nelson asked.

"That's complicated. At the time it was simple. Ethan had business practices that in the security world we saw as less than average," Dina said. "But now that I've done a deep dive, I've learned that Seth Baxter was whispering in everyone's ear that Marcus was working with a homegrown group to buy and sell government secrets."

"Holy shit." Nelson grabbed the tablet with both hands.

"It's believed that Seth and his team were intercepted and murdered by whoever he ratted out and that investigation is still ongoing." Louis leaned against the side wall and sipped his coffee. "Your mother has learned that Marcus, Chuck, Josh, and Tyler are all on the short list. What's even more interesting is that Tyler works for a company similar to Ethan's and Marcus is a major investor."

"And Ethan is on that company's board," Dina said.

"This is too much." Brandi flattened her hands on the table and rose on shaky legs. "Are you suggesting that Marcus and his friends killed Seth's SEAL team and that my ex-boyfriend might have had something to do with it?" She wrapped her arms around her middle.

"All the reports I've read don't indicate Ethan had anything to do with the actual deaths, but he's definitely in bed with Marcus." Dina nodded toward the table. "There are surveillance pictures taken of them together this past winter."

Brandi gasped.

Nelson rushed to her side.

She took a step back. "You're suggesting that Ethan used me to get to Nelson."

"We are," Louis said.

"I feel sick." She flattened her hand over her stomach. "Do you have any idea how insane this all sounds to me?"

"We do." Dina nodded.

"If it's true, he could have put a backdoor into our system," Brandi said. "That means he could have access to all our communications, which means he would know we've been onto him."

"You've discussed the manuscript in email?" Louis said.

"No." Brandi shook her head. "But we can share the document and notes inside our editorial system. That way my father, brother, and I can see what all our editors are doing. It's not to check up on them or anything, but a way to ensure privacy since we had a breach that caused a scandal with Lake a while back.

We used it to discuss the changes we wanted made so that we could see if Marcus was willing to make major changes to the story. It was our way to see if he was serious about being published, or if this was all a game."

"Sounds like Marcus knew you'd do that," Dina said. "I take it you discussed with Ethan how you'd use the system."

"We did." Brandi blew out a puff of air. "This entire thing was a setup from the very beginning, including Ethan wanting to get back together."

"You can't let that upset you," Dina said. "Marcus and his team have been working on this for a long time."

"I've always believed something else happened on that mission that I wasn't aware of." Nelson pulled her close to his body, holding her in his strong arms. "Marcus wanted me to take the fall for Seth's death."

"We believe that was always the plan," Dina said. "He gets rid of Seth and you at the same time."

"It makes a little more sense on why Roxy came to me that night," Nelson said. "If they had been able to prove I was at fault, I could possibly have motive to get rid of Seth."

"Another possibility is that once both teams were dead, they could find fault in the current system, pushing Ethan's," Louis said.

"This is worse than a bad movie script." Brandi

rested her head against Nelson's shoulder. "I've rejected books that sound less convoluted."

"At least now we know what we're dealing with." Nelson kissed her temple.

"So, what do we do now?" Brandi asked.

"We put the pressure on Marcus," Dina said. "Once he sees Louis and I are here and we make it clear it's not just for the movie premiere, he'll get really nervous. I mean a five-star general and someone from the Department of Defense? He'll start shifting his plan and we'll be ready."

"I don't want Brandi or anyone in her family to be collateral damage," Nelson said.

She glanced up. "Thanks to Ethan, I already am."

15

Nelson reeled up his line for the third time in the last ten minutes. He leaned over the side of the boat. The minnow was still attached to the hook. Releasing the tension, he dropped it back into the water.

"Relax, son." His father sat in the bow of the boat with his legs stretched out on the rail and his hat pulled down so it appeared he was half-asleep.

There were so many things Nelson wanted to say to his old man. Too many questions filled his brain and not enough answers. But every time he opened his mouth, his dad shut him down. Either it was because Brandi was in the room or he'd been told he'd have all the information he'd need in good time.

Nelson respected his father both as a parent and as a general in the Army.

Talk about infuriating.

"This is the first time since we opened that none of us is at Blue Moon." While he and his brothers had been concerned about leaving the restaurant for the first time with their management team, that was only part of his stress.

The other part was that Brandi wasn't at his side, and he didn't like it when he wasn't in control. Her safety was his responsibility. If anything happened to her, he'd never be able to forgive himself.

"Your mother is with her. They have backup. It's fine," his dad said.

Nelson glanced over his shoulder. Maverick and Phoenix sat in the stern seats, looking equally as miserable as Nelson felt. It had always been difficult to be the children of the great Louis Snow. They could never quite live up to his impeccable reputation at West Point, or anywhere they went in the military.

His dad always told him that he never expected his boys to follow in his footsteps, but if they made that choice, it was their responsibility to strive to be the best of the best.

The pressure had been ingrained in Nelson's brain from birth.

"It's about time you boys took a day off." His dad tipped his hat and smiled.

"That's rich," Maverick said. "Because doing a stakeout isn't work."

"We're fishing." His father yanked his sunglasses off and lowered his chin, giving them that fatherly stare that used to—and still did—scare the crap out of all of them. It wasn't just the glare from a father, but from a five-star general. "We're having father-son bonding time. It's fun."

Nelson did his best to shake off the feeling that he was eighteen again and had just received his first demerit at West Point. That had been a painful phone call to make to his old man.

"You can dress this up any way you like, but we're on a mission, Dad." Phoenix had always been the kid who pushed the limits, hard. He struggled with authority and it showed on his written evaluations. But in the field, Nelson would rather have either one of his brothers than anyone else. Phoenix might be a bit of a hothead, but he had a big heart and was all business where it mattered.

"Maybe so, but spending time with my boys is still nice." His dad nodded. "I haven't been up here since the grand opening of Blue Moon and we stayed at The Heritage Inn. I love that place. It's so pretty from the water, isn't it, boys?"

"You are so weird, Dad," Maverick said.

"This reminds me of Nelson's fourteenth birthday and we all went camping." Phoenix chuckled. "Dad made us fish every morning before he'd take us waterskiing."

"If I hadn't done that, we wouldn't have caught our dinner every night." His father jiggled the pole as if he had a bite, but it turned out to be nothing since he dropped the line further down to the bottom and relaxed back into his seat.

"We did eat a lot of fish on that trip," Maverick said. "All fried in bacon fat. I'm shocked we're all not dead from a heart attack."

Nelson couldn't bring himself to make the trip down memory lane. His mind was split between the fact his girlfriend was hanging out with his mother and the idea that his mom used her contacts to bring in her own resources. He twisted his body and reached for a soda from the cooler. He cracked it open and chugged half of it down before lifting his cell from the console.

No messages from Brandi.

He had no idea if that was good or bad. God only knew what childhood stories his mother was telling.

But also, there was nothing from Reese, Jared, or any other trooper under Jared's charge. And nothing from the private investigator still spending time at The Heritage Inn.

Hensley hadn't been able to find anything useful in her trips into Marcus' and his buddies' rooms. All their electronics were locked up in safes and she'd been unable to access them.

Although, now that Dina Snow and the power she brought from the Department of Defense had arrived, things had changed and Reese had been given the go-ahead from the United States Government to open those safes and hack into any computers or other devices they might find.

"Could at least look like you're enjoying yourself." His father stood and yanked at his pole. He cranked the reel. "Damn. He took a tug and swam away." He finished pulling in the line and rested the pole in the holder. Making his way to the stern, he squeezed Nelson's shoulder. "I know you're worried about Brandi and her family, but we're going to put an end to this before anything bad can happen."

"I don't understand why you waited hours to tell me Mom pulled in a JSOC team. Why did you feel the need to keep that secret?" Nelson glanced up at his father. "And how the hell did she make that happen anyway?"

His dad sat down next to him and let out a long breath. "The truth is this isn't completely sanctioned."

"What does that mean?" During his time in Delta Force, Nelson worked more than one JSOC assignment and at least half a dozen unsanctioned missions. All that meant was that if he failed, the military would deny any involvement and he could possibly be left out to dry.

But no one ever used the words *wasn't completely sanctioned* when it came to anything that flew under the radar. Either it was, or it wasn't. There wasn't anything in between.

"The JSOC team's involvement is something your mom arranged. It's not on the books, and it's not off the books. They are doing this because of their loyalty to me and your mother," his dad said. "The only thing we have the green light on is to be read in on the investigation, which is a bunch of bureaucratic red tape right now."

"I don't understand. They know Marcus and his crew could be committing treason," Maverick said. "Not to mention killed good men in the field."

"They don't have proof and they need to get it," his father said. "They believe the only way to do that is to watch EMS Security, Ethan, and all the other players. According to Mom's sources, the FBI is in the process of putting a plant in Ethan's company. They want to know where the flow of information is going. Who they plan on buying from and selling intel to. They are looking at the bigger picture. Not what happened when Seth died."

"I take it you and Mom didn't explain all that was happening up here," Phoenix said.

"I took time off to see my boys and she worked her magic in places this general doesn't even know about." His father lifted his cap and ran a hand across the top of his head. "The military wants to protect national security. That's their job. They need proof of what Marcus and his crew are planning on doing. They are entertaining talks with Tyler's company so they can gather their own intel. If they get involved with a tiff between you and Marcus that doesn't even appear to be an issue, it could prevent them from moving forward with their plans."

"Sometimes I fucking hate the government and the general military where it's mission over men," Nelson muttered. "It's why we all went Special Forces where it's often men over the mission."

"I understand." His father nodded. "Your mother and I both feel we can put an end to both problems. It's why she put her neck on the line with the JSOC team."

"Your job could be hanging in the air too, Dad." Nelson arched a brow. "You're a general. This could be seen as an act of—"

"You're my son and what happened to you has haunted me every day. If I lose my rank, I don't care. This is the right thing to do. Besides, I'm going to retire next year."

"Are you serious?" Nelson stared at his dad. "I never thought I'd see that day."

"Neither did I," Maverick said.

"How does Mom feel about that?" Phoenix asked.

"She's got one foot out the door as well."

Nelson's cell buzzed. He lifted it and glanced at the screen. "I got a text from Reese."

"What does it say?" Maverick asked.

"Hensley's successfully hacked into Marcus' computer. She's downloading the pertinent files onto a drive. Reese says we should all meet back at my place to discuss," Nelson said. "Let's pull up these lines and haul ass."

"Hey. How are you holding up?" Nelson stepped from his boat to the dock and took Brandi into his arms, giving her a quick kiss on the lips, ignoring the fact that his brothers and parents were standing a few feet away. He rubbed his hands up and down her arms.

"I'm a little freaked out, to be honest," Brandi said. "There's some guy in your kitchen with all this specialized computer equipment and he, Reese, Stacey, and Frank are going through it all, talking in hushed voices like they don't want me to hear any of it."

"There's a lot of sensitive information that my parents need to be careful with." He pressed his lips against her forehead. "But I'll make sure you're not kept in the dark where it matters."

"I'm scared." She blinked. "It sounded like Marcus and his friends were planning on doing something sinister at my mom's premiere party."

"Let's go inside and find out what's going on." He laced his fingers through hers and tugged her toward the steps that led up to the house.

His brothers and dad were two paces behind.

When he entered through the patio sliders, his mother stood behind a man sitting at the kitchen table who had set up a highly sophisticated laptop and other instruments that Nelson didn't pretend to understand.

Reese, Stacey, and Frank were gathered around the table, all looking at printouts. Both Frank and Stacey were in uniform.

Stacey lifted her gaze. "Welcome to the party."

"I'm ready to be briefed," he said.

The man at the computer glanced over his shoulder. "Is that wise with—"

"It's fine," his mother said. "Nelson, this is Boomer. He's also Delta Force and an expert in cyber security and IT."

Boomer stretched out his arm. "It's a pleasure to meet you and all your brothers. I've heard a lot about you from your mom."

"Thanks for coming," Nelson said. "What have you found?"

Boomer wiggled his fingers over the keyboard and tapped at a few screens. "It's a pretty elaborate plan and kind of ingenious."

Nelson leaned against the counter, keeping Brandi close. He could feel the fear seeping off her skin.

"The first thing Marcus planned on doing was wreaking havoc on the Grant Publishing computer system starting tomorrow. I'm working on making sure that it doesn't happen in the way that they planned."

"What exactly did they intend on doing to our system?" Brandi asked.

"Sending out massive emails where they didn't belong," Boomer said. "Things like private emails between editors about writers and then sent to authors. From rejection letters to the wrong recipients. Things like that. Anything to make you all scramble to fix the problems."

"That would make us call Ethan." Brandi leaned closer to Nelson, holding on to his arm with a death grip. "That would fall on me."

"They knew that." Frank waved a piece of paper in the air. "The idea is to force you back to New York City to meet with Ethan to fix the errors and then—"

"Kidnap her?" Bile filled Nelson's throat.

"Not exactly," Stacey said. "They are running on the assumption that Nelson has his hackles up."

"That's an understatement," Phoenix muttered.

"They assume that Nelson would leave with Brandi, which is a mistake. That leaves only two Snow boys to deal with." Stacey shuffled some papers around.

"If I were to have left, that means someone else would have to take over helping to make sure everything is in place for the premiere." Brandi glanced up at Nelson. "That would get put on Leslie and her team."

"You mean Roxy," Nelson said.

"Exactly. And her role would be to sabotage the premiere." Boomer shifted the screen.

"She wouldn't be allowed to be alone in your restaurant," Maverick said. "So, that wouldn't work."

"Oh, but they have some plans for the brothers." Boomer shifted the screen. "Things like rigging home security systems to go off and they have the capability."

"Ethan is a genius when it comes to shit like that," Brandi said. "In college, he would hack into systems to prove how unsafe they were and then show the businesses how he could help them. He's mad wicked smart."

"Curiosity killed the cat." Nelson rubbed the back of his neck. "How did they plan on ruining the premiere?"

"Bad food. People getting sick. Movie equipment breaking down. Anything to make Nelson and his brothers look bad," Boomer said. "But that's just the beginning. It's all meant to look as though Nelson did it in a fit of jealousy."

"Now why the hell would I do that?" Nelson asked.

"Because they were going to make it look like Ethan and Brandi were carrying on behind your back and tie it all back to when you supposedly killed Seth because Roxy wasn't going to leave him after you slept with her and she got pregnant," his mother said.

Nelson turned and slammed his fist on the

counter. "You've got to be fucking kidding me." It was so ridiculous it would probably work.

"I wish I was." His mother rested her hand on his back. "But none of this is going to happen. Not on my watch."

Nelson pressed his hands on the cold quartz top and sucked in a deep breath. He'd made a million and one mistakes in his life, but nothing compared to the night he hadn't turned Roxy away. His stomach churned. "Had I not slept with her, they'd never be able to do this to me. Or to Brandi."

"That's not true," his father bellowed. "They never used that against you until now; honestly, they could still do all this without the affair."

"That's bullshit," Nelson mumbled.

"No. It's not." Brandi took his hand. "The only way this doesn't work is if I hadn't gone back to Ethan over the holidays. All they need is for you to appear to be jealous. It doesn't matter if you aren't or never were. If I hadn't done that, this plan falls apart."

"You both need to stop beating yourselves up over this," his mother said. "There are five contingency plans. This is just the one that played out."

Nelson turned and gave his mom a weak smile. Dwelling on the past wasn't going to solve the present problem. "What do you propose we do from here?"

"I'm glad you asked that question," his mother said. "But you're not going to like my suggestion."

Brandi sat on the edge of Nelson's bed and stared out the sliding glass door. Like the Fourth of July, the moon and stars lit up the dark sky. In the distance, she could see boat lights on the lake. Normally, a night like this would be calming.

Nelson eased onto the mattress and wrapped a loving arm around her waist and kissed her shoulder. "I'm so sorry," he whispered.

"I'm the one who should be apologizing." Tears burned the corners of her eyes. "Deep down, I knew getting back together with Ethan was a mistake. If I'm being honest, I did it because I was scared of what I was feeling for you."

He took her chin with his thumb and forefinger. "We had no commitment to one another. You owed me nothing."

"That's not the point." She pushed his hand away and stood. "Ethan constantly asked me about my love life. If there had been anyone special. If I had been seeing anyone. He even asked if someone was in Lake George."

"But you never told him about me."

"That almost makes it worse." She tucked her hair behind her ears. "Maybe if I had, I might have realized sooner what you meant and I wouldn't have let things go on as long as they did. I feel so foolish."

"I understand."

She glared. "Do you?"

He tilted his head. "I slept with a married woman using me to get pregnant, so she and her brother could use that against me. Of course, I do."

She dropped her face into her hands, letting out a guttural sob. "You can't make this shit up."

"No. You can't." He tugged her to his chest, pressing his warm lips against her forehead. "What happened in the past is over. We can't do anything to change it. All we can do is move forward and make sure we stop them from ever hurting anyone again."

She lifted her gaze. "Do you really think this plan your mom has come up with will do that?"

"My mother runs some serious black ops for the government. Even my dad, the general, will admit she's smarter than he is when it comes to planning and executing a mission. My mom wasn't Special Forces in the military because she's a woman."

"That's sexist and I can't imagine she took that sitting down."

He laughed. "She went through all the training that I did, but because of the way the armed forces are, they would never give her the chance to be a team leader the same way my father was, or I was. So, she used her unique skill set behind the scenes and my father helped her find government operations that would utilize her talents."

"Your parents are pretty cool."

"I tend to agree, only being their kid can be hard.

Sometimes me and my brothers feel like we disappointed them when we left the military and came up here to run a restaurant."

She palmed his cheek. "I spent all afternoon with your mother. She's quite proud of you and everything you've done, including Blue Moon."

"She said that?"

"Among other things."

"Oh yeah? Like what?" He slid his hand up under her shirt, fiddling with the clasp on her bra.

"She told me that being in Delta Force had been your entire life and after the doctors told you that you'd never be able to go back to that life, she and your dad worried how it would affect you."

"I did think my world was over." He lifted her shirt over her head. "Phoenix felt the same way. His injury also pulled him out of the field."

"Your mom told me that Phoenix had been looking to transfer into an administrative role." She tilted her head. "When you left, it was easy for him to follow you."

"Boy, my mom certainly gave up some family secrets." He leaned over and kissed the center of her chest. "It's nice to know she and my dad see that running a business makes me happy."

Brandi giggled.

He lifted his gaze. "What's so funny?"

"Oh, I think her exact words were, *Every time I spoke with my boy, I felt like he was going through the motions of living. Then he started talking about some girl named Brandi and he sounded like the day he got accepted into Ranger School. That's when I knew you stole his heart."*

Nelson blinked. "My mother said that?"

"I choked on a strawberry and thought she was going to have to perform the Heimlich maneuver."

"Both my parents can be blunt." He moved his lips to her belly as he tugged her jeans to her ankles. "But she's right. As much as I love owning Blue Moon with my brothers and living here in Lake George, I love you more." Gently, he pushed her to the mattress.

Her heart hammered against her chest.

He stood at the edge of the bed and removed his clothing. His gorgeous body shimmered in the moonlight.

"I love you," she whispered. Her breath hitched.

"Good, because I'm never letting you go again." He eased his hard body on top of hers, gently lowering his weight as he stared into her eyes. "I promise I will protect you, always." His mouth brushed over hers tenderly.

She couldn't think of a time in her life when she felt more loved and cared for by a man. Nelson represented everything she could have ever wanted. Ever dreamed of. He'd come into her life when she'd least expected to fall in love, and yet, he'd been exactly what she'd been looking for.

He was kind, considerate, and the most loving creature she'd ever met. He loved her like she was the most important person in his life. He treated her with respect and more importantly, he'd been open and honest where it mattered the most.

It scared her how quickly they'd fallen in love and much she'd come to need him in her life.

She savored every touch of his hands. Every kiss of his lips against her skin. He knew exactly what she wanted. What she needed. What she desired.

And he didn't hold back.

Settling between her legs, he thrust deep inside.

She arched her back, accepting his length, begging him to bring her over the edge.

He lifted his chest from hers, bringing his hand between their bodies, finding her hard nub and rubbing gently as their bodies rocked together in the purest form of love.

Holding his gaze, she let her orgasm take over. Her body shivered. Her toes curled. Her lungs burned as she gasped for breath. "Oh, God. Yes."

He buried his face in her neck, moaning as his climax slammed against her, exploding like a million firecrackers.

Her vision blurred. "Nelson," she whispered. "I love you."

"I love you back." He collapsed to the side, pulling her with him, holding her tight, his fingers dancing up and down her spine. "Do you think your dad's going to let you move a satellite office up here sooner? Because long distance is going to suck."

She laughed. "After meeting you and seeing us together, he's softening on the idea."

"I'm glad I made a good impression. I've been worried they were going to hate me because of all this."

She propped herself up on his chest. "They told me they can see why I've fallen in love with you."

Both Nelson's brows shot up. "You told them you love me?"

"I didn't have to. They could see it."

16

Nelson stood in his office, staring out the window overlooking the bar area. The first part of the plan had been put into play.

Now it was a waiting game.

He'd learned that patience was his friend when he'd been in the field, but waiting had never been easy.

It got worse now that the woman he loved could end up being put in danger. He pressed his hand against the center of his chest. He'd served in battles with every member of his family and the fear of losing his parents or his brothers wasn't something foreign to him, but this feeling was something entirely new.

He wasn't sure how to deal with it other than he knew without a shadow of a doubt if he ever lost

Brandi, a big piece of him would die, and he'd never heal from that.

The door to the office opened and Maverick stepped inside. "Ethan was picked up by the FBI," he said. "He hasn't rolled over yet, but it's going to be hard for him to deny what he's done."

Nelson turned. "Any news on Marcus and his crew?"

"It doesn't appear that Ethan or anyone from his company sent Marcus a message," Maverick said. "The Grants' charter plane landed in NYC and Mom's at their offices. Last I heard, Ethan was about to enter the building. Brandi's father is at The Heritage Inn talking with Leslie as we speak, making a stink about something happening with the computer system and how Brandi left to fix it."

"I don't like that I'm stuck up here, and she's at Foster's rental house." Nelson rubbed the back of his neck. He'd snuck into his restaurant before opening and had been hiding in his tiny office ever since. No one knew he was there, except Veronica and the three JSOC team members who were pretending to be new hires for the movie premiere. He had to do whatever was necessary to keep his staff safe, which meant keeping them in the dark.

Maverick leaned against the wall and folded his arms. "We need your eyes here when mine and Phoenix's security alarms go off, and we have to leave to pretend to deal with that. We have to let all this play out."

Nelson didn't need his brother to go over the plan and all the whys with him, but he did appreciate Maverick trying to calm his nerves.

"Once we see what Roxy does on the inside, we'll have more to take to Mom's team," Phoenix added.

"We still need Marcus and the rest of his cronies." It killed Nelson on how Marcus kept one step on the fringe, using his sister to do some of the dirty work. "If only we knew more about Tony and Joe."

"We do," Maverick said. "One of Dad's buddies is talking with them right now."

"Nothing like burying the lead, little brother."

Maverick shrugged. "They might not know anything of relevance. They were only on Marcus' team for six months and their after-action report of the mission didn't have any revealing information other than their request to transfer came before the mission in question and that Marcus and three other team members had been MIA for a few hours." Maverick held up his hand. "It was explained later the team had been out for drinks at a local bar."

"In a hostile country?" Nelson had heard this part of the story months after his release from the hospital in Germany and it always struck him as odd. Not that it couldn't have happened since he and his team had often dealt with downtime by blowing off steam much in the same way. Not to mention that Marcus wasn't there on a rescue mission. He'd been in the area for something entirely different.

"Yeah, that's another thing that Dad learned that we didn't know until this morning."

Nelson cocked his head. "What's that?"

"Marcus volunteered his team—actually, begged—to go to that location for a recon mission. He and his team had been there months before and they felt they had a good handle on whatever situation they had been assessing."

"That didn't have to do with Seth's team?"

"Nope, but Marcus must have known where Seth's deployment was and did his best to get close to the region," Maverick said. "Anyway, it's highly suspect that Tony and Joe weren't included in the outing, which tells us they probably didn't know what was going on." Maverick pulled his cell phone out. "It's Dad."

"Put it on speaker."

"Hey, Dad. You're on speaker with Nelson."

"Ethan just rolled. He's singing like a canary," their father said. "We have Tyler and Marcus on corporate sabotage. So, we have two choices. We can have the FBI pick them up now or continue with the plan."

Nelson rubbed the back of his neck. "How ironclad are the charges?"

"There is always the chance they walk," his father said. "We keep going, and we might we get them on treason and that would be the better outcome. Either way, we've at least got this to fall back on and the FBI is letting Mom make the call, so in reality, Nelson, this is your decision."

"Hang on. Let me text Brandi." He pulled out his phone.

"Is that really necessary?" his father asked. "I know you're in love with her, and we adore her, but—"

"This affects her just as much as it does me." Quickly, he sent a text to Brandi, giving her a succinct update.

Bubbles appeared immediately.

He held his breath.

Brandi: *I'll do whatever you think is best, but since you asked my opinion, don't you think going for it all is better? Wouldn't you rather be vindicated? I know I would.*

God, he loved that woman.

"Let's nail this bastard to the wall."

"They're doing what?" Nelson leaned back on his desk and pinched the bridge of his nose.

"You heard me," his father's voice bellowed through the cell phone. "Something or someone tipped them off."

"We figured that when the alarms on Maverick's and Phoenix's houses didn't go off, but why would they pack up and leave? Something doesn't feel right. Marcus doesn't quit."

"Maybe not, but he's proved to be patient."

"He also had more than one contingency plan. Why isn't he falling back on those?"

"I'm betting they will be, but they need a moment to regroup," his father said. "It looks like Roxy is staying behind, so Hensley will stay put to watch her, and one of your mom's men will follow Marcus."

Nelson shifted his gaze to the ceiling. "Is the FBI still pressuring Ethan?"

"They are," his father said. "So far, all Ethan has given them is what he did with Grant Publishing and several other companies. He hasn't given up much on Tyler's company yet, and that's what they need."

"I can get that for them." Nelson let out a long breath.

"No, son. I'm not letting you use yourself as bait."

"It's the only way to end this once and for all." Nelson wasn't going to let his father talk him out of it. "I'm heading to The Heritage Inn now." He tapped the red button. He strolled to the other side of his desk, opened the top drawer, and pulled out his revolver. He holstered it before snagging his keys.

A month ago, he'd have walked out of Blue Moon and gone into battle without thinking twice.

Now he had someone in his life who made him think about more than himself. He found Brandi's contact information and hit the call button.

It rang once.

And in the middle of it, his father tried to call back. He sent it straight to voicemail.

"Hey, you," she said. "What's going on?"

"Nothing good," he admitted. "Who's with you?"

"Why? What's happening?"

"Marcus and his crew are packing up and I'm not going to let them leave."

"Nelson, what are you going to do?"

"Confront this head-on," he said. "Now, answer my question, please."

"One of your mom's men is here. He comes in the house every so often to tell me it's all clear and then goes back outside."

"Tell him that stuff is happening and to keep an eye out."

"I don't like this. You're putting yourself in danger."

He raced to the door and took the steps into the restaurant two at a time. Veronica called to him, but he ignored her. His mother tried to call, but he didn't answer. "The only way to end this is to get Marcus to admit what he did and what he's planning. Trust me when I tell you that he's arrogant enough to toss that in my face if he thinks he's got me by the balls." His phone buzzed. This time it was Maverick.

Shit.

He didn't have time to deal with each member of his family trying to talk him out of this.

"I love you," he said. "Stay safe."

"Nelson, please—"

"Brandi. Trust me."

"It's not—"

"I've got to go." He pulled open his truck door. "I'll call you when it's over." Time to put the past where it belonged.

In the rearview mirror.

Brandi closed her eyes and tried to keep the tears from flowing down her cheeks.

It didn't work.

She swiped at her face, leaning against the back of the sofa in the middle of the family room. She blinked, staring out the big picture window overlooking the lake.

There were so many details she didn't understand. Things that didn't make sense. But she did get that Marcus was dangerous and wanted Nelson out of the picture.

Permanently.

And he didn't have any problems making sure that happened.

The sound of the front door jiggling made her jump. She gasped. It shook again. She glanced at her watch. Neptune, the man who had been assigned to this detail, came inside about every twenty minutes.

It had been eighteen since the last time.

She shook out her hands. There were military people everywhere. She was safe.

The door flung open and a different man—a familiar one, but he wasn't Neptune—stepped inside holding a large rifle. He pointed it directly at her chest.

"Hello, Brandi," Tyler said. "Good to officially meet you."

Every muscle in her body froze. Her throat tightened. She tried to swallow, but couldn't. No words formed. Not even a scream. She stood there, unable to move. Unable to do anything.

Her thoughts went to Nelson and what trap he must be walking into. Her fear turned to anger. "Where's Neptune?" she managed.

"If you're asking about the man outside, he's of no concern to you anymore."

"You killed him?" She gripped the couch.

"If it helps, I didn't want to." Tyler smiled. "Now, let's go."

"Where are you taking me?"

"You'll find out soon enough." Tyler inched closer. The barrel of his rifle was still pointed at her chest, and he had a wicked grin plastered on his face. "Do as you're told, and you won't meet his same fate."

"And what about Nelson?"

"His fate was sealed the first time he died."

Nelson checked his weapon before easing from his truck and heading toward the cabin where Marcus had been staying.

"Nelson," his father called from somewhere behind him.

He turned.

"They're gone," his father said.

"Give me the location." Nelson wasn't going to let this go. He needed it to end.

His father raked a hand across his head. "We lost them."

"You what?"

"They split up half a mile from the hotel." His dad shook his head. "They pulled into the convenience store parking lot down the street and hopped into four vehicles. We weren't prepared for that. We were only able to follow two."

"Jesus," Nelson muttered. "And where are those two?"

"Marcus and Chuck are heading up Assembly Point."

"That's where my house is."

His father nodded.

"You have no idea where the other two are?"

"We don't."

"And Roxy? Is she still here?"

"No. Leslie took her to Blue Moon. Otherwise, I

wouldn't be showing my face out in the open," his dad said. "I tried calling you to tell you what was going on."

Nelson pulled out his cell. "I need to warn Brandi."

His father's strong hand came down on his shoulder. "I just got word from Mom."

Nelson's heart dropped to his toes. He stared into his father's unwavering gaze.

"Her detail was taken out. She's missing."

"You've got to be fucking kidding me." Nelson kicked the gravel. "How the hell did that happen?"

"We played into—"

"It was a rhetorical question, Dad." Nelson turned and planted his hands on his hips. "They have to be taking her to my house." He turned on his heel. A strong hand curled around his biceps. "We can't go in without a plan."

"I'm not going to just stand here and do nothing. They have my girl and what they really want is me."

"They want you dead and if you go in there half-cocked, they are not only going to kill you, but they will kill her too."

"Fuck." He knew his father was right. He could handle his life ending, but he couldn't allow them to take Brandi's. That wasn't going to happen on his watch.

"Marcus knows you care about Brandi. He's expecting you to run in all hot under the collar. But what he doesn't know is that Mom and I are here. He doesn't know that the man who was watching Brandi was from a JSOC team."

"He might know that Ethan was compromised and is talking with the FBI."

"That's true, but that doesn't change his plans with you. Thinking all that through, in his mind, he can still get away with it because according to what we've gotten from Ethan, one of the contingency plans was to use the short relationship she had with him as fuel to some jealousy you might have had," his father said.

"I've never been a jealous man."

"It doesn't matter. You love her and that changes things. Look at how you're acting right now. You're ready to go in there, with no backup, to end this because of her. He was banking on that."

His father had a point.

"Look. Jared has pulled as many of his troopers as he can. We outnumber them on land and by water. We need to take the time to do this right."

Nelson nodded. "All right."

His father rested both hands on his shoulders. "We've got Marcus and his crew on a litany of shit and he's going down. You will finally be able to live your life without this shadow hanging over your head."

17

Brandi tried to twist her hands, but the duct tape was too tight. Her feet were tied to the chair. Even if she tipped it over, she couldn't free herself. Not that she knew anything about being held hostage. The only experience she had was in books she'd edited. But that was fiction. It wasn't real.

However, she conjured up every heroine she'd ever read that had been in this situation.

There were better courses of action than waiting for her hero to come and save the day.

Marcus and Tyler sat at the island while Chuck stood watch on the patio and Josh was out front.

She had no idea if Nelson had learned yet that she'd been kidnapped, but she had to believe that was part of Marcus' grand scheme.

Though it seemed like a stupid one.

Everyone would know.

Wouldn't they?

"I have a question," she said. Maybe talking to her captives would help.

Marcus glanced over his shoulder. "And what's that?"

"What do you plan on doing with me?"

"That's easy. You're bait to bring your boyfriend to me," Marcus said.

"What then? And how do you plan on getting away with it?"

Marcus laughed. "That's simple. You had an affair with your ex-boyfriend. We have the pictures. This will be a crime of passion." Marcus lifted his hand, made a gun sign with his fingers, and held it to his head.

"That's never going to stick." She swallowed. "No one will believe that. Besides, your friend there already killed someone. How is that going to be explained?"

"Nelson did it," Marcus said.

"Why would he do that?"

Marcus shrugged. "Who knows? But you'll be dead, so no one will pin it on us. Problem solved."

"You really are an arrogant asshole if you think anyone will believe that bullshit."

Marcus' phone rang. "It's Nelson. Tape her mouth shut."

She gasped.

Tyler took more duct tape and smacked it across her face.

She groaned.

"Hello?" Marcus set his phone on the table in front of her, as if to taunt her. "Nelson? Is that you?"

"Where's Brandi?" Nelson's voice hit her ears like a warm blanket.

She twisted and moaned, trying to make noise, but it wasn't enough.

"She's a little tied up right now." Marcus smiled. "But she's fine."

"If you hurt her, I will kill you."

"I doubt that." Marcus eased onto one of the chairs. "You have a beautiful home."

"You broke into my house. I should call the cops."

"That would be a *grave* mistake." Marcus rolled his fingers on the table.

It grated on Brandi's already shot nerves.

"I would appreciate a face-to-face conversation. Perhaps we could clear up a few things."

"I'll be there in ten."

"Come alone, or you won't be happy with the outcome." Marcus ended the call. "Tyler, tell Chuck and Josh to be ready."

Nelson rested his cell on his knee as he turned the corner onto Assembly Point. "How's the hack into my security system coming?"

"Boomer's almost done," his father said. "He'll need your phone on so it can connect for at least three minutes once you're at the front door."

"I'm sure they will greet me at my truck before I even depart the vehicle. Is there a plan B to listen in? Because I'm sure Marcus will check me for a wire and shut down my phone."

"Everything in your house has been disabled. We do have a court order, so Boomer is working on a secondary solution to get the system running, but that will take a little longer, and we won't have any way of letting you know we've been successful."

"Except when you come storming in," Nelson mumbled. "What if I leave my phone in the truck? Will that be close enough range?"

"I don't know. It will be best if you bring it in."

Nelson slowed as he approached his driveway. "I'm here. Got to go." He tapped the end button and stuffed his cell in his pocket, putting it out of sight.

The sun had begun its descent behind the mountains. The darkness would become his team's friend.

Jared, Stacey, and Reese were in the water.

His parents and brothers were flanking from the south, and the rest of his mom's JSOC team was coming from the north.

Neptune's body had been located and his mother

personally wanted to wring the neck whoever pulled the trigger.

She'd have her day in court.

As soon as he shut the engine off, he was greeted by Chuck, who shoved a rifle in his face.

"Hand over your weapon," Chuck said.

He pulled it from its holster and placed it in Chuck's hand. "You're still in the military, right?"

"I have one more tour left," he admitted. "Same with Josh."

"I hate to be the one to tell you this, but it's going to end in a dishonorable discharge and probably prison time."

Chuck laughed. "Make yourself at home. Oh wait, this is your home." He gave Nelson a little shove with the wrong end of the rifle. "Marcus is waiting for you in the kitchen."

Nelson made his way to the front door, where he curled his fingers around the handle and sucked in a deep breath and counted to ten.

"What are you waiting for?" Chuck called.

Nelson pushed open the door and slowly made his way through the family room and headed toward the kitchen. He stopped dead in his tracks when he locked gazes with Brandi.

Her beautiful green-blue eyes were wide with fear. Her mouth was taped shut, hands tied behind her back, and her feet were duct-taped to the chair legs.

"You fucking bastard," Nelson muttered. He made two tight fists.

"That's no way to greet an old friend." Marcus sat at the table with a gun in his lap and pointed it at Brandi. "Join us."

"Untie her."

"Not going to happen just yet."

"At least take the tape off her mouth." Nelson pulled up a chair.

"Before we do that, I need to make sure there are no wires."

Nelson lifted his shirt.

Marcus nodded. "Now hand over your cell."

This was exactly what they anticipated. Nelson reached into his back pocket and set his phone on the table.

Marcus snagged it and shut it down.

Hopefully, it had been long enough for Boomer to work his magic. If they could get into Nelson's security system, they could listen inside the house. Now all he had to do was keep Marcus talking.

"Now can I take the tape off Brandi's mouth?"

"Sure, why not, but it's going to hurt." Marcus waved his weapon.

"I'm sorry, sweetheart." Nelson inched closer, gripping the side of the adhesive. He tugged gently.

She flinched.

"Are you ready?" Nelson asked.

She nodded.

Like a Band-Aid, he ripped it off in one quick motion.

"Ouch. Jesus, that hurt." Brandi opened and closed her mouth.

Nelson leaned over and kissed her tenderly. "Sorry I had to do that."

"Aw. Aren't the two of you cute." Marcus rested his gun on the table. "I never expected that Brandi would believe your side of the story."

"What is that supposed to mean?" Nelson asked.

"I thought once she read the book and put it all together, she would have backed away slowly, realizing what a snake you were for sleeping with a married woman." Marcus tapped the weapon against his chest. "I didn't consider the fact she'd fallen in love with you. I had only wanted to use this as a way to mess with you. To toss you off your game so Roxy could come into the restaurant and mess up the premiere party, make you look bad, and eventually, you would have wound up dead." Marcus shook his head. "Now I have to kill both of you."

That right there should be enough to bring in the cavalry. That was if they'd been able to take out Chuck, Josh, and Tyler.

Patience.

"You're never going to get away with it," Brandi said.

"But I already have." Marcus leaned back. "Me and my friends have checked out of the hotel. We've left the area. No one knows we're still here. No one will believe it was us. We've been nothing but kind to Nelson. I've extended one olive branch after the other. He's the one who has been acting delusional."

Nelson laughed. "I suppose some people on the outside looking in could view things that way, but no one in my family would see it that way."

"Of course not. They are biased."

"Nor mine," Brandi chimed in.

"And there is this added issue with Ethan and his company," Nelson said. "Did you know the FBI picked him up for questioning? Something about cyber breaches with Grant Publishing. I heard he's giving them all sorts of information."

Marcus' lips drew into a tight line. "That has nothing to do with me and has no bearing on this situation."

Out of the corner of his eye, Nelson saw movement across the back patio and it wasn't either of Marcus' buddies. "Oh, but I think it does, especially when he's taking an immunity deal and rolling over on Tyler's company."

"I'm done with this conversation," Marcus said. "Time for a crime of passion that ends in a murder-suicide."

The sliding glass door opened, and Maverick appeared.

"What the hell?" Marcus jumped to his feet, his

weapon waving wildly in the air, a little too close to Brandi.

Nelson stepped in front of Marcus.

Bang!

Brandi screamed.

The front door flew open. The sound of boots hitting the tile floor hammered Nelson's eardrums.

A sharp pain seared through his side. He grabbed his gut and looked down. Blood trickled through his fingers. "Fuck." He dropped to his knees.

Someone's foot flew in front of him, smashing Marcus right in the nose.

"You motherfucker." Phoenix wrestled the gun from Marcus' hand before tackling him to the ground. "Can someone untie Brandi? I don't think Nelson is in any shape to do it."

Nelson fell backward, clutching his side. He blinked, staring up at his mother.

"Why are you always the one getting shot?" His mom grabbed something from the counter and pressed it on his stomach.

Hard.

"Jesus, that hurts." Nelson tried to take in a deep breath, but the pain hit his brain like a cattle prod.

"Just relax." His mom brushed his hair from his forehead.

"Brandi?"

"I'm right here." She dropped to her knees, taking his hand.

"Are you okay? Are you hurt?"

She shook her head. "I'm fine, but you're not looking so good." She wiped a tear from her cheek.

"Good," he managed.

"He's losing a lot of blood," his mother said. "How far out is the ambulance?"

"Five minutes," he heard his father say.

More voices filled the air, but he couldn't distinguish them anymore. The pain turned to a dull ache. He knew that sensation well. He sighed and closed his eyes.

"No," Brandi said. "Stay with me."

"I'm not going anywhere. I love you." And then the world went black.

Brandi paced in the emergency room. It had been hours since they wheeled Nelson into the operating room.

"You might as well sit down and relax," Dina said.

"I don't know how you all can be so calm." She plopped down on the hard chair beside her mother, who looped an arm around her, tugging her close.

"Sadly, this isn't our first rodeo," Louis said.

"Hopefully, it's our last." Dina arched a brow.

"He's going to be fine." Her father patted her knee. "The doctors said it was a straightforward surgery."

"That's not exactly what he said." Brandi rested her head against her mom's shoulder and closed her eyes. Every moment she'd ever spent with Nelson filled her mind. Every tender kiss. Every kind word. She'd fallen so hard for him, and she wanted to spend the rest of her life showing him how much he mattered.

She allowed her brain to wander into the future and what life might be like with Nelson. If they ever moved in together. Or got married.

Maybe even had kids and what they might look like.

Her chest tightened.

Her life wouldn't be as full without Nelson in it.

"Hi, Jared," Louis said.

She blinked her eyes open and forced herself to stand. Her muscles felt weak as if they couldn't hold her weight. Her father took her by the arm.

"I spoke with the local FBI officers, and they will be taking over from here," Jared said. "Everyone is in custody, and I heard that Ethan will be given special treatment for his testimony regarding Tyler's company and what his plans were for buying and selling of military secrets."

"It sucks that he's getting off," Brandi said.

"He's not." Jared looped his fingers in his belt loop. "He will lose his company. He'll be fined a shit ton of money for his crimes, and he'll never be able to work in this field again. He will feel pain for what he did."

"I guess that should be good enough." Brandi sighed. The embarrassment of being taken in by him still filled her heart. If she hadn't allowed him back in her life, perhaps she could have at least put a dent in his plan. However, she couldn't dwell on that now. She needed to send positive energy to Nelson. All her thoughts needed to be with him.

"Brandi, the doctor's here." Her father squeezed her shoulder.

She turned. "Is Nelson okay? Did the surgery go well? Did you get the bullet out?"

The doctor clasped his hands in front of his body. "Yes to all of those questions." He nodded. "He's going to need to stay here for about three or four days, but he'll be as good as new in about a month."

"Oh, thank God," Dina said with a big sigh. "If he ever gets shot again, I'll kill him myself."

"You'll have to stand in line." Louis wrapped his arm around his wife, kissing her temple.

"He's in the recovery room. He's quite groggy but awake. You can all see him, but I don't want to exhaust or overwhelm him," the doctor said.

"Why don't you go see him, darling." Dina rested her hand on the small of Brandi's back. "I'm sure you're the first face he'd want to see."

"He's your son. You should—"

"Go," Louis said. "We're going to go grab a bite to eat with your parents. We'll see him later."

"Are you sure?" Brandi wiped the tears that burned a path down her cheeks.

"We're sure." Dina smiled.

She squared her shoulders and followed the doctor through the double doors and down a long corridor.

"Don't stay too long. He needs his rest." The doctor pushed open a door. "Ever since he woke up, he's been talking about you. He's a lucky man."

"I'm the lucky one." She inched into the room. The sound of machines beeping filled her ears. She swallowed.

Nelson lay on a gurney with an IV in his arm pumping fluids and probably pain medication into his system. A machine flashing his vitals was on the other side. Not that she knew much, but she understood enough that his were good.

He turned his head and blinked. "Hey, good-looking." He lifted his hand and wiggled his finger. "Come sit."

"You gave everyone quite the scare." She eased onto the side of the mattress and rested her hand on his thigh. "The bullet just missed your spine and some important organs. It could have been a tricky surgery."

"So I've heard." His voice sounded raspy and weak. "How long have I been out of it?"

"It's six in the morning."

"Wow," he said. "What was the final outcome? Everyone taken into custody?"

"Jared said the FBI is taking over, but that it's a solid case and Marcus and his friends will be going away for a long time," she said. "I must admit, I feel bad for Marcus' wife. She's pregnant and will have to raise that baby alone."

"That is unfortunate, and I wish things were different for her, but I have no regrets for Marcus going to prison."

"I don't either." And that was the truth.

"The doctor said I'm stuck here for a while and will miss your mom's premiere party."

"My mom wants to push it off until next weekend. She and Leslie are working out the details." She took his hand. "Maverick and Phoenix said they can make the adjustment."

"Of course. Anything for your family." He reached for her, tugging her closer, and groaned. "Shit, that hurts."

"You need to be still."

He lifted her hand to his lips. "I'd take a bullet for you any day."

"Let's hope you never have to do that again." She leaned forward and brushed her mouth against his in a slow, tender kiss. "I love you, Nelson."

"Not as much as I love you."

EPILOGUE

FOURTH OF JULY

Brandi leaned against the post and stared at the clear blue sky. The sun hovered just above the mountaintops, beginning its journey into night. She lifted her glass of wine and took a slow sip, savoring the rich flavor. The last couple of months had been a roller coaster. There had been interviews with local law enforcement, the FBI, and even the military.

All ending up with Marcus and his crew facing treason charges.

Nelson had been vindicated. His past completely cleared of any shadow hanging over his head.

Her father had been agreeable to giving Edward more responsibilities and allowing Brandi to work at least two weeks a month remotely in Lake George. Her love for Nelson grew with every waking moment.

"There you are."

She glanced over her shoulder and smiled.

Nelson had jogged down the steps as if he'd never been shot. His recovery had been lightning fast and he had no lasting issues from the incident. The doctors had been worried there could be some problems down the road, but Nelson had not a single one.

"Everyone has been wondering where you disappeared to." Nelson came up behind her, wrapping his arm around her middle, and kissed her neck.

"I needed a moment alone."

"I know what you mean. Our families can be overwhelming when they get together."

"I'm glad they all enjoy each other's company." She set her glass on the post and turned. "I can't believe both your parents are retiring."

"And moving up here." Nelson took her chin with his thumb and forefinger. "They have this wild idea that we're going to get married and give them grandbabies."

"I know. Your mom told me five times today how beautiful I look with my niece in my arms and wouldn't it be wonderful if I had one of my own."

"I was holding Foster and Tonya's baby, and my mom told me that I'd be a natural father." Nelson laughed.

"You are the baby whisperer."

"I wouldn't go that far." Nelson took her by the hand. "Let's go for ride in the rowboat. My dad is

JEN TALTY

going to set off some fireworks. It will be nice to see them from the water."

"Shouldn't we watch them from shore with everyone else?"

"I want some time alone with you." He helped her onto the small vessel.

His romantic and spontaneous side always surprised her, but she wasn't about to complain. She belonged in his arms and that's where she intended to stay.

She settled between his legs as he rowed away from the dock. The sun had completely disappeared and the sky turned a deep dark blue. The stars came out and the white moon hung high. She could see their families gather on the deck and Nelson's father light the first of the fireworks.

"Wow," she whispered. "That's so pretty."

"My dad loves this stuff."

"So do I." She leaned back, resting her head on Nelson's chest, and watched as his father lit up the sky. It wasn't anything like what was to come when the village put on the major event of the night, but it was a nice start.

She squinted, watching Maverick and Phoenix roll open something the size of a large sheet. "What are your brothers doing?"

"Helping me propose."

"What?" Her heart jumped to her throat. She stared at the white sign as someone flashed a big light on it. The words *Will you marry me?* appeared in bold letters.

Nelson held a diamond ring in front of her nose.

Her breath caught in the middle of her chest. "Nelson," she managed. "What have you done?" She twisted and palmed his cheek.

"I love you and I want to spend the rest of my life proving it to you. Will you do me the honor and be my wife?"

Tears burned a hot path down her face. "Nothing would make me happier."

He took the ring and placed it on her finger. "My mother was right."

Brandi tilted her head. "About what?"

"Us getting married and having babies."

"Don't tease, because I'm going to want one of those sooner rather than later."

"I'm not joking. I'm forty years old. No time like the present to get working on that."

She smiled. "Let's kick everyone out." Wrapping her arms around him, she kissed him, hard. In the distance, she could hear cheering and shouts of congratulations. She'd found her happily ever after and she was never letting go.

ABOUT THE AUTHOR

Jen Talty is the *USA Today* Bestselling Author of Contemporary Romance, Romantic Suspense, and Paranormal Romance. In the fall of 2020, her short story was selected and featured in a 1001 Dark Nights Anthology.

Regardless of the genre, her goal is to take you on a ride that will leave you floating under the sun with warmth in your heart. She writes stories about broken heroes and heroines who aren't necessarily looking for romance, but in the end, they find the kind of love books are written about :).

She first started writing while carting her kids to one hockey rink after the other, averaging 170 games per year between 3 kids in 2 countries and 5 states. Her first book, **IN TWO WEEKS** was originally published in 2007. In 2010 she helped form a publishing company (Cool Gus Publishing) with *NY Times* Bestselling Author Bob Mayer where she ran the technical side of the business through 2016.

Jen is currently enjoying the next phase of her life… the empty nester! She and her husband reside in Jupiter, Florida.

Grab a glass of vino, kick back, relax, and let the romance roll in…

Sign up for my [Newsletter](https://dl.bookfunnel.com/82gm8b9k4y) where I often give away free books before publication.

Join my private [Facebook group](https://www.facebook.com/groups/191706547909047/) where I post exclusive excerpts and discuss all things murder and love!

Never miss a new release. Follow me on Amazon: amazon.com/author/jentalty

And on Bookbub: bookbub.com/authors/jen-talty

ALSO BY JEN TALTY

Brand new series: SAFE HARBOR!

MINE TO KEEP

MINE TO SAVE

MINE TO PROTECT

Check out LOVE IN THE ADIRONDACKS!

SHATTERED DREAMS

AN INCONVENIENT FLAME

THE WEDDING DRIVER

CLEAR BLUE SKY

NY STATE TROOPER SERIES (also set in the Adirondacks!)

In Two Weeks

Dark Water

Deadly Secrets

Murder in Paradise Bay

To Protect His own

Deadly Seduction

When A Stranger Calls

His Deadly Past

The Corkscrew Killer

Brand New Novella for the First Responders series
A spin-off from the NY State Troopers series
PLAYING WITH FIRE
PRIVATE CONVERSATION
THE RIGHT GROOM
AFTER THE FIRE
CAUGHT IN THE FLAMES
CHASING THE FIRE

Legacy Series
Dark Legacy
Legacy of Lies
Secret Legacy

Emerald City
INVESTIGATE AWAY
SAIL AWAY
FLY AWAY

Colorado Brotherhood Protectors
Fighting For Esme
Defending Raven
Fay's Six

Yellowstone Brotherhood Protectors

Guarding Payton

Candlewood Falls

RIVERS EDGE

THE BURIED SECRET

ITS IN HIS KISS

LIPS OF AN ANGEL

It's all in the Whiskey

JOHNNIE WALKER

GEORGIA MOON

JACK DANIELS

JIM BEAM

WHISKEY SOUR

WHISKEY COBBLER

WHISKEY SMASH

IRISH WHISKEY

The Monroes

COLOR ME YOURS

COLOR ME SMART

COLOR ME FREE

COLOR ME LUCKY

COLOR ME ICE

COLOR ME HOME

Search and Rescue
PROTECTING AINSLEY
PROTECTING CLOVER
PROTECTING OLYMPIA
PROTECTING FREEDOM
PROTECTING PRINCESS
PROTECTING MARLOWE

DELTA FORCE-NEXT GENERATION
SHIELDING JOLENE
SHIELDING AALYIAH
SHIELDING LAINE
SHIELDING TALULLAH
SHIELDING MARIBEL

The Men of Thief Lake
REKINDLED
DESTINY'S DREAM

Federal Investigators
JANE DOE'S RETURN
THE BUTTERFLY MURDERS

THE AEGIS NETWORK

The Sarich Brother

THE LIGHTHOUSE

HER LAST HOPE

THE LAST FLIGHT

THE RETURN HOME

THE MATRIARCH

More Aegis Network

MAX & MILIAN

A CHRISTMAS MIRACLE

SPINNING WHEELS

HOLIDAY'S VACATION

Special Forces Operation Alpha

BURNING DESIRE

BURNING KISS

BURNING SKIES

BURNING LIES

BURNING HEART

BURNING BED

REMEMBER ME ALWAYS

The Brotherhood Protectors

Out of the Wild

ROUGH JUSTICE

ROUGH AROUND THE EDGES

ROUGH RIDE

ROUGH EDGE

ROUGH BEAUTY

The Brotherhood Protectors

The Saving Series

SAVING LOVE

SAVING MAGNOLIA

SAVING LEATHER

Hot Hunks

Cove's Blind Date Blows Up

My Everyday Hero – Ledger

Tempting Tavor

Malachi's Mystic Assignment

Needing Neor

Holiday Romances

A CHRISTMAS GETAWAY

ALASKAN CHRISTMAS WHISPERS

CHRISTMAS IN THE SAND

Heroes & Heroines on the Field

TAKING A RISK

TEE TIME

A New Dawn

THE BLIND DATE

SPRING FLING

SUMMERS GONE

WINTER WEDDING

THE AWAKENING

The Collective Order

THE LOST SISTER

THE LOST SOLDIER

THE LOST SOUL

THE LOST CONNECTION

THE NEW ORDER